The Sunset Job

Rainbow's Seven Duology - Book One

Max Walker

Edited By: ONE LOVE EDITING

Cover character illustration by Karina Budnariu

Cover designed by Max Walker

Copyright © 2022 by Max Walker

All rights reserved.

No part of this book may be reproduced in any form or by any electronic or mechanical means, including information storage and retrieval systems, without written permission from the author, except for the use of brief quotations in a book review.

Wyatt Hernandez is working a dead-end tech job at the Miami Science Museum, struggling to support himself and his sister. An expulsion from Yale University made him largely unemployable and left him uninspired and utterly lost.

Roman Ashford is working different "jobs" and raking in the cash. But one job promises the biggest reward yet. In order to complete it, he has to assemble a crew: the Rainbow's Seven.

Roman is at six out of the seven when he goes to Wyatt for help, knowing how skilled the freckled-face man is behind a computer. He explains it's a heist that would have them traveling the world, promising riches beyond belief.

If they succeed.

It might have been an easy choice for Wyatt, if only Roman hadn't been the primary reason behind his expulsion—along with being his first and only love.

Things grow more complicated when a rival group shows that they'll stop at nothing to finish the heist first. Suddenly, more than the success of the job is on the line. The crew will be put through a series of harrowing tests, and so will Roman and Wyatt's second-chance at a happily ever after.

Also by Max Walker

The Gold Brothers

Hummingbird Heartbreak

Velvet Midnight

Heart of Summer

The Stonewall Investigation Series

A Hard Call

A Lethal Love

A Tangled Truth

A Lover's Game

The Stonewall Investigation- Miami Series

Bad Idea

Lie With Me

His First Surrender

The Stonewall Investigation- Blue Creek Series

Love Me Again

Ride the Wreck

Whatever It Takes

Audiobooks:

A Hard Call - narrated by Greg Boudreaux

A Lethal Love - narrated by Greg Boudreaux

A Tangled Truth - narrated by Greg Boudreaux

A Lover's Game - narrated by Greg Boudreaux

Christmas Stories:

Daddy Kissing Santa Claus

Daddy, It's Cold Outside

Deck the Halls

* * *

Receive access to a bundle of my **free stories** by signing up for my newsletter!

Tap here to sign up for my newsletter.

Be sure to connect with me on Instagram, Twitter and TikTok **@maxwalkerwrites.** And join my Facebook Group: Mad for Max Walker

Max Walker

MaxWalkerAuthor@outlook.com

Chapter 1

Wyatt Hernandez

A GAGGLE of uniformed children burst through the bright red doors and into the Miami Science Center, crowding around a table that was meant to show how tides worked, water funneling in from one end and covering the fake beach to the intense excitement for the gathered fourth graders. One of their chaperones came over to Wyatt Hernandez and drew his attention up from the computer screen, her dark green nails tapping rhythmically across the white countertop.

"Hi, sir, I was just wondering at what time the Planetarium Show starts?"

Wyatt tried his hardest not to glance at the massive sign that hung above her, the words "Trip Around the Galaxy Show: Every hour on the hour." twinkling across it as if written in stars. The skylights around the sign opened up to a cloudless blue expanse, the sun beaming through the glass.

"It starts every hour and lasts fifteen minutes. I'd suggest getting there five minutes before so you can get everyone settled in."

"Perfect, thanks so much." She offered a friendly smile and turned, looking up at the sign and muttering something under her breath before working to wrangle the class.

Wyatt got back to reading the gossip article that filled up his screen, clicking through the annoying slideshow of information and battling a hundred different pop-ups, all to find out that the actress and rock star ended up divorcing amicably.

He rolled his eyes and clicked out of the article, opening another window displaying lines and lines of code. This was really the only reason why he stayed in this job, the fact that he could sit and work on his side projects without anyone stopping him. It certainly wasn't because of the pay or the people, that was for sure. He could have made more managing an IT department somewhere, but that would mean he'd have actual responsibilities and eyes over his shoulder, making it much harder for him to work on his side projects.

So he stayed, surrounded by the chatter of excited kids and the slumped shoulders of the exhausted adults.

Today, he worked on an app idea that wouldn't

function the way he wanted. He could normally handle a couple of bugs with his eyes shut and one hand tied behind his back, but something must have happened early on in the code and cascaded outward, creating a tangled web of brackets and letters and numbers. He cracked his knuckles and dug in, feeling the usual thrill that came with a complicated coding problem unfurling in front of him.

"Excuse me."

Wyatt's eyes drew up from the screen and landed on a bright smile. The woman in front of the desk appeared as if she had her own personal spotlight shining down on her, her raven-black hair perfectly framing an angular face with pouty lips and eyes crowned with orange eye shadow.

"Hi, yes, how can I help you?"

The woman leaned forward and dropped her voice so that Wyatt also had to lean to hear her. "I'm assisting a celebrity with a top secret music video they're shooting. I can't say the name, or I'm pretty sure the NDA magically appears and suffocates me, but I promise you've heard of them. You might even be part of the hive."

Wyatt perked up, that last word serving as a juicy hint. "Would you like me to call our events manager?"

"Actually, I've worked with Gina before, back when she was at the Natural History Museum. If you could just unlock the door to the offices, I can go and have a chat with her." She shot a hurried glance at her gold wristwatch. "It's time-sensitive."

"Right, of course, let me just call ahea—"

"No need," she said, reaching across the desk and placing a soft hand on Wyatt's, pushing it off the phone. "I talked to her yesterday. She's expecting me."

Wyatt chewed the inside of his cheek. His inner voice was riddled with anxiety about getting in trouble with the higher-ups, which likely came from his experience of getting thrown out of college. It had left him with a permanent weight of anxiety every time he thought about upsetting any authority figures. And letting an unauthorized guest through a locked door that held not only administrative offices but also storage rooms for highly valuable and irreplaceable items was definitely listed as a "no-no" somewhere in the employee handbook.

The woman must have sensed his hesitation. She clicked open the strap on her black leather purse and pulled out her phone. A moment later and she was speaking, no longer in hushed tones. "Hey, B, yeah, we might need to scrap the—I know, I know how much this means to you. What about—right, of course. No, I thought the staff would be aware. Can you—"

Wyatt got up, keys jingling in his hand. "It's okay. I'll walk you to her office."

The Sunset Job

There, problem solved. He'd escort her all the way to Gina's office and explain everything there. He walked around the wave-shaped desk and motioned toward a nondescript door next to the sandpit. A man stood with his broad back to them, turning for a moment and revealing a face covered by impenetrable sunglasses and a dark red cap sitting low on his head. He turned away, as if the display explaining the importance of tides was the most interesting thing in the world.

A distant bell of familiarity rang in Wyatt's head. He couldn't really focus on it, though, since that was the exact moment the door opened and out walked Gina Perez, her tight brown curls bouncing on her shoulder, nearly as bubbly as Gina's personality was.

Wyatt waved, grabbing her attention. "Hey, Gina, I was just heading toward your office. This woman here was requesting to speak with you."

"Hm? Who?"

"Her," Wyatt said, turning and realizing he never even got the woman's nam— "She's gone."

Except he saw her, walking out of the sliding glass doors and into the main entrance hall of the Science Center. She was different, though, no longer with short black hair but instead sporting brunette waves that fell down her back.

Why the hell was she wearing a wig?

"What was it about?" Gina asked, puckering her

lips, her polka-dotted skirt blending with the pink-and-white floor.

"I'm... well, I'm not entirely sure. She wanted to talk to you about using the museum for a music video. It was kinda sketchy, though."

Gina shrugged and squeezed Wyatt's elbow. "Please don't get me assassinated, okay? I've got a lot of secrets." She tapped a red fingernail against her temple and giggled, walking around Wyatt and down the hall toward the cafeteria. Wyatt chuckled and started back toward his desk. He'd completely lost track of where he was in the string of code that filled the computer screen, but it would only take him a couple of seconds to pick it back up again.

The perks of being a techy savant.

And then, before he could even sit back down, everything went to hell in a handbasket.

A loud bang erupted in the room, followed by three seconds of ear-ringing silence. The eerie quiet was shattered by a shriek and a shout.

"Gun!"

Chaos broke out as everyone in the sunshine-soaked room bolted toward the exits, creating a crush of terrified parents and chaperones shielding their tiny, crying charges. They were all running from the three men standing in the center of the room, the tallest of them holding the gun up over his head, the two flanking him with guns of their own pointed in opposite directions.

The Sunset Job

Wyatt froze. He'd never seen a gun in person before, never been this close to a life-ending push of the trigger. He should be running, ducking for cover, crawling toward an exit. Instead, he just stared, jaw split open, pupils blown wide with fear.

A body slammed into him, sending them both to the ground. The impact was shielded by the two big arms that encased Wyatt, keeping his ribs buffered from a hard hit against the floor. The man rolled on the floor as two shots rang out, bringing them both behind a stone column.

"Stay down," his savior said, and the bell of familiarity suddenly rang even louder than the bullets that exploded from the guns. He looked up, the man with the sunglasses and hat no longer a mystery to him.

"Roman?" Wyatt asked, shocked he could even say his name out loud.

The man took off his sunglasses and smiled, devastatingly nonchalant for the incredibly shitty situation they were knee-deep in. He pulled out a gun from under his shirt and stood up, back against the column.

"It's been a while, Wyatt. You're looking good."

And before Wyatt could even process the words coming from the ghost standing above him, Roman cocked his gun and leaned around the column, aiming and shooting, the bullet hitting its target and shattering a shoulder. The man dropped to his knees with an anguished cry, letting go of the gun he was holding to push against the bleeding wound instead. Suddenly, another loud shot rang through the room, and the man to the left of the tall one dropped like a fly, holding his calf and curling into a ball, the pink-and-white tiled floor swirling with red.

"Nice shot, Bang Bang," Roman said, stepping out of cover, leaving behind an incredibly shocked and insanely scared Wyatt wondering why the hell his old flame turned archnemesis had just saved him from being shot in the head?

Chapter 2

Roman Ashford

ROMAN ASHFORD WAS the kind of guy who believed in staying ready so he never had to get ready. When he planned today's job, he had accounted for some interference by making sure Bang Bang had his back covered. He was hoping it wouldn't come to a shootout in the middle of a science museum, but it looked as if that was exactly what was about to happen.

"Nice shot, Bang Bang," Roman said, stepping out from behind the column and aiming his gun directly at the only man left standing.

"Eh, I was aiming for the left leg."

Bruno "Bang Bang" Vázquez was the ordinance expert of the group with a sharpshooter's eye and an almost religious reverence for firearms. He was using his "Sunsplitter" today, a brightly painted yellow SIG M17, with sparkling rays of burnt orange shooting down the barrel. He loved customizing his guns and had even been known to cover some of his bullets in glitter, too. The mountain of a man was an *extra*-fabulous kind of killing machine, with an affinity for drag queens and football and a heart the size of the sun.

Roman always felt at ease having him by his side. Especially today.

"Leonidas Thorn, drop your gun." Roman spoke directly to the man left standing, a cocky smile splitting his face like the scar that ran down the side of his head, the white of his scalp slashing through the dark black hair. A golden necklace holding a lion's tooth hung down toward the center of his chest. A perfect bullseye for Roman to target.

"Nice job, Roman." Leonidas slowly crouched, midnight-black eyes pinned on Roman's gun. He set his pistol down by his feet, hands raised above his head. "Thought I got rid of you in Brazil."

"And I thought we were better friends than that."

"This how you treat all your friends?"

Roman shrugged, walking over and kicking the pistol away from Leonidas. "Just the ones I really like." Bang Bang came up behind Leonidas and pressed the barrel of his golden gun into the back of the man's neck. "Looks like Bang Bang really likes you, too."

The other two guys continued to squirm on the floor, one of them quietly whining as blood pooled around his leg. Roman gave the one on the left a kick, silencing the whimpering for a moment. He knew there wasn't much time left before this place was surrounded by SWAT. He had to get what—and who—he'd come for before that happened.

"You'll never find it, Roman. Not before I do. You know that, so why are you even trying?"

Roman smiled, licking his lips and leaning in. He could count each individual pore on Leonidas' face, could see the tiny wrinkles and folds around his eyes and forehead, could see the flecks of light blue inside the sea of navy that surrounded his pupils. Reflected back was the bottomless pit full of crime and sins committed by the scarred man.

Leonidas Thorn, head of a ruthless criminal organization called the Pride, made up of bloodthirsty predators looking for an easy ride to the top. Roman had crossed paths with them before

"Because I've already found it, friend. And I'll be able to open it with the key I'm about to walk out of here with."

Leonidas couldn't control the twist of shock that briefly contorted his expression. "Bullshit. No one knows where the money is."

"No one *knew* where the money was. Past tense, buddy. Maybe crack a book instead of a skull next time." Roman glanced out the sliding glass doors that led to a sun-soaked atrium. A security guard was running toward them, gun drawn. This entire job was blown the second Mimic couldn't get into the back.

Artemis 'Mimic' Flores, one of Roman's closest friends and most trusted allies. She was a human chameleon, able to blend into any situation or scenario that landed in their laps. She wasn't only good about disguises for herself, either. She had a knack for dressing up and making others look unrecognizable.

Roman saw when she had to back out, understanding that shit was about to hit the fan. She had left just as the Pride made their entrance.

He looked over his shoulder at the column hiding Wyatt. There could still be a way to salvage this.

"End it," Roman said, speaking around Leonidas and directly to Bang Bang.

"You got it, boss."

Leonidas chuckled, eyes narrowing to slits. "You aren't the only one with friends."

Before either Roman or Bang Bang could react, a high-pitched hissing sound filled the space. A smoke grenade rolled against Roman's feet, instantly covering the area in a dense gray cloud of smoke.

"Shit, Roman, I can't see."

Bang Bang lost his shot. The one chance they had at wiping out the leader of the Pride and making their lives a hell of a lot easier. He should have taken the shot himself, but he had no time to regret it. He only had enough time to get him and his crew the fuck out of there. When the smoke cleared, Roman saw that Leonidas was gone, and the two men at their feet had their throats slit, their whines replaced by a few dying gargles.

"Fuck," Roman said. "Go to the car."

"You sure?"

"Go," he said to Bang Bang, turning back to the column and running around it. Sirens announced the arrival of law enforcement. He had about two minutes or less before the place was surrounded.

"Wyatt, you okay?"

The glasses-wearing blond kid with the near-perfectly symmetrical freckles Roman had known since he was fourteen looked up at him, brown eyes blown wide with fear underneath the magnifying lenses of his Ray-Bans. He had the sudden urge to grab him in a tight bear hug and tell him it was all going to be okay, even though he really had no idea if that was the truth or not. He also wanted to wrap an apology into that bear hug.

"No, no I'm fucking not okay. What in the actual hell is going on?"

"I can explain it all later." He put a hand out, helping Wyatt get back onto his feet. His entire body warmed at the touch but was instantly cooled off by the way Wyatt recoiled away, snatching his hand back as if reeling from a burning stove.

This next bit would be the hardest part of the job: convincing Wyatt to come with him.

"We don't have time." Roman could hear the whir of a helicopter through the shattered glass. "Wyatt, I need your help. It's part of the reason why I came here. I wanted to ask under different circumstances, but I've got zero control right now. You're an absolute fucking savant when it comes to computers, and I don't think I can finish this job without you. So, please, help me, Wyatt."

He blinked a couple of times, mouthed a couple of near-words before actually being able to put a coherent sentence together.

And that sentence was "Absolutely fucking not."

The helicopter was directly overhead now. No time left. Roman considered—for a flash of a second—just grabbing Wyatt by the arms and throwing him over his shoulders, lugging him out of here like a caveman carrying away a slab of meat. He quickly realized that would be crossing over the line into kidnapping territory, which was *not* how he wanted this partnership to start off. He knew Wyatt already hated his guts, his parents' guts, his grandparents' guts, his Viking ancestors' guts, and anyone else's guts who was somehow tied to Roman Ashford. It radiated off the guy, as if Roman had thrown open the doors to a furnace, heat blasting his face. Wyatt's fists bunched at his sides. He was a lean guy, always had been, but Roman was surprised to see some definition in the biceps that filled his sleeves.

Time had changed him, but it didn't diminish the obvious anger that Wyatt hadn't let go of.

And Roman didn't blame him, either. What happened between them was immensely fucked-up and had likely changed the trajectory of both their lives. But he wasn't about to grovel, beg Wyatt for forgiveness. There were very few reasons for Roman to get on his hands and knees, and apologizing was *not* one of them.

He'd have to figure something else out.

"Alright, fine." He started toward the door that led out to the gardens. Wyatt had a hand on his head, a slight tremor apparent in his shoulders. Wyatt's shoulders always shook when he was nervous or overwhelmed. Roman used to call them his little saltshaker. Wyatt didn't like that too much at first, but it ended up growing on him.

"I'm sorry," Roman said, wishing things had turned out differently for them. Before Wyatt could respond, Roman turned and ran, throwing open the door and bolting toward the fence, grabbing two iron rings and launching himself over the curved spikes, landing in a roll on the other side.

"Took you long enough," Bang Bang said as he opened the passenger door to a sleek emerald-green BMW.

Roman gave his best friend a pat on the back of his neck and got into the car, Bang Bang sitting in the back seat. Monica "Mustang" Mercedes sat behind the wheel, her expression as casual as a soccer mom waiting in the school's pickup lane.

"Got what we came here for?" she asked, kicking the car into drive.

Roman answered with a single shake of his head. It was enough. Mustang nodded solemnly, dropping a pair of Oakleys on her face and zooming out of the narrow alleyway. She swerved out onto a wide street lined with palm trees and blended right into the traffic heading toward Miami Beach, police officers racing in the opposite direction.

Roman looked into the rearview mirror, the science museum getting lost behind a cruise ship, and wondered how the fuck he was ever going to finish this job now.

Chapter 3

Wyatt Hernandez

WYATT REMAINED in a state of shock for hours after the police were gone, the dim haze of adrenaline and fear slowly lifting by the time he got out of the hour-long shower, his bathroom filled with steam. He could smell the pizza his sister had warmed up for him, but his stomach made an uneasy flip and directed him away from the kitchen toward his bedroom instead. He threw himself facedown on the squeaky bed, a couple of rebel springs poking at his ribs.

"Wyatt? Everything okay?" It was his sister, leaning into his room with a slice of pizza in hand.

Why does everyone keep asking me that.

"Yeah, everything's fine."

"I highly doubt that." Julie came and sat down on the edge of the bed, the thin mattress loudly complaining about the added weight. "You told me work was crazy today. You didn't tell me there was an entire shoot-out in the middle of the museum."

"I was going to tell you. Just didn't want you to worry."

Julie scoffed at that. She was younger than Wyatt by three years but always acted as if she had ten over him. And rightfully so. She'd been the one to hold it all together after their parents passed; at only fifteen years old, Julie had taken the wheel and guided both her and her brother back to a semblance of their old life—pre-helicopter crash. It took Wyatt some time to regain his footing, having been dealt with the loss of his parents and the loss of his promising career all within months of each other.

"How'd you find out?" Wyatt asked.

"It's all over the news. No one's said a motive or anything yet. Just that men with guns stormed the museum." Julie shook her head, and Wyatt could see her bottom lip quiver with the impending crash of tears. "Guns, Wyatt. Were you near them when it all happened?"

Wyatt could see the nightmares already beginning to take shape behind his sister's eyes. He decided skirting the truth would help more than hurt in this situation. "No, I wasn't. I was safe. It all happened so fast, anyway. I still can't really believe it."

Julie wrung her hands so that the tips turned

cherry red. "Did they take anything? Or was it like a gang thing?"

"Both, I think. There were two groups there, must have been after the same thing. No idea what that was, though. I can't think of anything we have in the museum that would cause a freaking Wild West shoot-out." Echoes of gunshots rang through his skull. Images played across his vision like a broken reel: blood, smoke, more blood, two men with their throats flayed open, even more blood. His stomach flipped again, and he was forced to close his eyes to stop the room from spinning.

Except closing his eyes only gave the images a cleaner canvas to work from. The back of his eyelids became projectors, the lifeless corpses staring back at him.

He snapped his eyes open. The room would have to keep spinning.

"Roman was there."

Julie's head snapped to face her brother, her honey-gold eyes wide and her bottom jaw hanging open. "Roman Ashford?"

"The one and only." Wyatt let his head drop against the wall, gaze floating up toward the popcorn ceiling, to the crack creeping across the corner where the white paint had turned brown from water damage. The upstairs tenants not only enjoyed playing soccer in the dead of night using bowling balls, but they'd also caused three leaks and set off five fire alarms in the two months that they'd been there.

"What... what was he doing there?"

Wyatt shrugged and let out an exasperated sigh, that question having stuck to him like a thorn through skin. He had a couple of guesses as to what Roman had been up to since they last spoke but nothing in the way of solid answers. From the way he was throwing around commands, it seemed like Roman had been the man in charge, but what the hell was he in charge of?

And what did he need Wyatt's help with?

Julie stood up and paced a small circle into the beige carpet. "Have you guys talked since everything happened?"

"Nope, not a single word. Not until today, after he tackled me to the ground and saved me from getting shot in the head."

"Jes—Wyatt! Really? How bad was it in there? Don't lie to me."

He filled his lungs with a deep breath, the oxygen feeling like a gulp of fresh water in the middle of a desert. "I don't think I was ever really in danger. They were there for something, and I don't think either group wanted to leave behind a big body count getting it. I just don't think they were expecting to be there at the same time. It messed everything up."

"And how did you feel? Seeing him again?"

Wyatt avoided his little sister's gaze. She knew just how badly Roman had hurt him, having been the one to comfort Wyatt after everything began falling apart. He'd fallen hard for the tall kid with the green eyes and effortless grin, his best friend and secret crush. Except it didn't stay secret for long, when they both drunkenly made out with each other at their high school graduation party. Wyatt had already come out to Roman but never told him about the feelings he had for his best friend. He was shocked when Roman confessed to having those same butterfly-farm-in-his-chest kinds of feelings. Not just because he thought his friend was straight, but because he assumed that even if he wasn't, he'd still be out of Wyatt's league.

Roman Ashford had everything going for him and everyone chasing after him, orbiting him like vultures eyeing a sun-dried meal. Beyond the fact that he had radiated confidence and charisma, he was also a gorgeous specimen of human. Tall and muscular and angular, with perfectly straight teeth and big lips that begged to be kissed, he was the definition of an attention stealer, able to control an entire room with a smile alone, going from perpetually baby-faced to smoldering sex symbol in a matter of seconds. Add to that the fact that the guy was a genius, especially when it came to chemistry and physics, that it seemed nearly impossible for anyone to match Roman's level.

"It didn't feel great, that's for sure. Especially not under the circumstances. If it wasn't for him, I wouldn't even be working a dead-end tech job at the museum. I could have afforded us both a nice bayside condo by now if—whatever, it doesn't matter." Wyatt rubbed a hand over his face and looked out the narrow window, seeing his neighbor eating noodles on the couch and watching *Maury*, nothing on but the red-and-white plaid boxers he'd been wearing for the last three days.

"You haven't dated anyone since him."

"I'm very much aware of that fact, Julie. I haven't had time. When I'm not at the museum, I'm working on my own projects, trying to make something that'll get us out of this cockroach-infested dump. It's got nothing to do with Roman."

Or the fact that Wyatt had a Roman-sized hole left in his heart after that stormy night on the boat that had changed everything.

Yeah, his barren dating life definitely didn't have to do with that.

The doorbell dragged him out of his thoughts. Julie looked to him, thin brows inching together. "Did you order food?"

Wyatt shook his head. "I was going to grab a slice of pizza in a second."

"Weird, I wasn't expecting anyone." Julie got up and went toward the door, but Wyatt rolled off his bed and cut her off, telling her to wait in the room.

The Sunset Job

He couldn't quite explain why, but the tingling sensation at the base of his neck made him feel extremely uneasy. Too much crazy shit happened in the past twenty-four hours for Wyatt to let his guard down.

He walked barefoot across the cool tiles, seeing the outline of a person's shadow from the drawn curtains. He looked through the peephole, a hand on the doorknob. The face that stared back at him wasn't one he recognized. He wasn't a police officer, either, judging by the all-black outfit the man had on, a necklace hanging down his chest with what appeared to be a shark tooth.

No, that's not a shark's tooth. That's a claw. A lion's claw.

Dread flushed through him, freezing his muscles and locking him in place. The men at the museum wore the same kind of necklaces. Wyatt would never forget seeing them on their dead bodies as he was escorted out of the crime scene by police, one of the officers mentioning the bloody claws.

Julie. I need to keep her safe.

That thought hit him like lightning, burning off the ice that had momentarily encased his entire body. He turned and ran across the living room, running to the hall, making it to his bedroom door just as the men outside grew impatient, one of them ramming the thin plank of wood with the force of an NFL quarterback, blowing off the hinges and sending the lock flying, landing right at Wyatt's feet.

"Stay inside, and don't open this door for anything," he said to a cowering Julie before throwing his bedroom door shut and shielding it with his body.

The cinder block of a man casually waved a gun in Wyatt's direction. "Wyatt Hernandez, put some shoes on, and let's fucking go. You're Pride property now."

Chapter 4

Roman Ashford

STEAM FILLED THE BATHROOM, covering the window that normally had a clear view of Miami Beach. Roman padded across the white-and-black marble, dripping water as he toweled off his hair. He left the wet towel hanging off the counter and went for the neatly organized row of face creams and lotions, squeezing a dollop of lightly scented cream onto his palm and rubbing it into his face, closing his eyes and letting the tingly mint settle into his skin.

It was a slice of calm, a peaceful ritual, much needed after the disastrous outing at the science museum.

Roman *hated* when things didn't go his way. He was used to solving problems before they even came up, able to see where something could and would go wrong while also coming up with a hundred different ways to get around the problem. He'd saved a job in

Morocco when he realized they were being double-crossed and another job in Italy that would have ended in his and his crew's fiery funeral if he hadn't figured out their hideout had been infiltrated and rigged to blow. It's part of what made Roman so cut out for the leadership role; not only was he able to lead into danger, but he was also able to lead away from it.

Except for today. He should have known the Pride would be as close to finding the key as they were. He thought he had at least a day's lead after he left them a false trail, sending them searching for the key somewhere down in Peru while Roman and his crew went to the real location.

He was wrong, and now he worried about what else he'd gotten wrong. How close was Leonidas to getting the book and ending this wild chase? He was comforted in the fact that Leonidas had to turn tail and run, same as Roman had, both of them equally empty-handed in their escape.

There was one advantage Roman had over Leonidas: knowledge that the key they were both hunting was only half of the puzzle. They'd need someone to decode the key, and that someone was supposed to be Wyatt Hernandez, Roman's old flame and biggest mistake. Not that Wyatt was a mistake—that was an impossibility. But meeting him, falling desperately in love with him, and then shattering his heart into a tiny million pieces

The Sunset Job

certainly qualified as a massive mistake in Roman's eyes.

He figured the hardest part of this entire job would be to get Wyatt on his side, and he knew it would take more than a single question asked moments after gunshots blasted through the air. Roman would have to prove he not only needed him but that he wanted to make up for the fucked-up shit he'd done, and what better way to do that than give Wyatt the chance at being a billionaire.

In his bedroom, Roman went to his walk-in closet and pulled out a black shirt with gray shorts, laying them out on the bed before going to his underwear drawer and taking out a navy blue jockstrap. He slipped those on, looking out the floor-to-ceiling window framing a picturesque view of gentle blue waves and a cloudless summer sky, the beach packed with rainbow umbrellas and sunbathing tourists. A cruise ship made its slow crawl across the horizon while a small plane advertised a foam party at a nearby club.

Roman finished getting dressed, slipping on his favorite Rolex—silver with a ruby-red face—just as his phone started to ring.

"Hey, Phantom, what's up?"

Axle "Phantom" Phillips was the crew's locksmith, a professional at breaking through any closed door or sealed vault. He worked as if he were an ethereal being, able to just walk on in like a ghost passing through a wall. Roman recruited him two years ago for a heist that found them in an underground safe surrounded by ancient mummies, one of them holding on to an insanely valuable diamond-and-sapphire necklace. Axle effortlessly got them through five checkpoints and three reinforced steel doors that were equipped with optical locks and biometric readers, making it seem like malfunctioning children's toys.

"Mustang is getting impatient. Wants to know when you're coming down."

"Does she have somewhere else to be?"

"Not sure. Think so—she keeps texting someone and smiling. I think she's setting up a date—"

The phone was snatched from Phantom, Monica 'Mustang's voice replacing his. "Roman, I'm not setting up a date. I'm talking to Alejandro."

Roman froze, sneakers hanging from his hand. "Your Pride contact?"

"That's the one. He says they're on the move, but they're not going after the book. They're going after something else. Someone else."

"Who?"

"He wasn't sure, just said Leonidas switched up their orders at the last minute."

Roman's gut twisted. This didn't bode well, not at all. He thought back through the events of the day, replaying conversations and scenes on fast forward.

Did Leonidas figure out the other reason Roman was at that science museum?

He threw on his sneakers and ran, hurrying down the hall and slamming a palm against the elevator's call button. "I'll be right down." He hung up the phone and stepped into the elevator, next to a woman in her bright pink bathing suit holding a Pomeranian in her hands, which was *also* wearing a matching pink bathing suit.

"Hey, Roman, you look a little frantic. Everything okay?"

Franny lived directly above Roman, having introduced herself three separate times on the day she was moving in. She enjoyed pointing out the obvious while being oblivious to it all at the same time.

"Just work stressing me out. Same shit, different day."

"You're telling me. I spent all morning getting into verbal boxing matches with my internet's tech support people and then found out my favorite Cuban deli down the street is closing, so I'm going to have to find a new place to sit and sip my cortadito. I think Saturn is having a retroascension... or is it a retro... retro..."

"Retrograde?"

"*Yesssss*, Saturn's in retromade, which—and I read this in my spiritual guide's handbook, so it has to be true—means we're all fucked. Isn't that fun?"

Roman considered getting off on the fifth floor

and just running down the stairwell, but he stayed on, tuning Franny out, his mind whirring back to Wyatt's scared but determined face after turning down Roman's request for his help.

The elevator doors opened into a mirror-encrusted lobby, with sleek furniture and potted palm trees flanking the front desk. Walking through the decadent space never failed to give Roman a flush of gratitude, briefly reminding him of the trailer park days that he had dug himself out of.

Sure, his money may not have been the cleanest, but it all worked the same once the cash was deposited.

Mustang was waiting in a neon pink Audi, the engine purring even as it idled. Roman jumped in the passenger seat, and Mustang was off seconds later, tires screeching as they searched for tread on the smooth pavement. Phantom leaned forward, hands on the seat, his smile reflected back at him through the rearview mirror. He wore a blue Marlins shirt and a matching blue cap flipped backward.

"Where we headed?" Mustang asked.

Roman rubbed his chin, calculating about a dozen different answers to her question. Only one of them made the most sense to him. "Drive toward Wynwood. Let's go to Wyatt's place. I want to check up on him."

"Got it."

Mustang had tailed Wyatt earlier in the day after

Roman asked her to keep an eye on him. She had reported that all was quiet by him, but things changed at a second's notice, and he didn't want to take any chances.

He's not going to be happy when I knock on his door.

Roman couldn't quite believe they were racing down a Miami highway heading toward the home of a man he thought he'd never see again. A man he couldn't get out of his dreams (and sometimes nightmares), someone whose memory was surrounded by what-ifs and "why us."

If Leonidas did anything to you...

Mustang swerved out of an exit and maneuvered down tight city streets, made even more compact by the cars parked alongside the road. The sidewalks were equally packed, with people walking up and down the art-filled street, the bars and restaurants filled to the brim.

As they continued to speed west, the restaurants and tattoo shops morphed into single-family homes with overgrown lawns, sandwiched between apartment buildings that desperately needed a fresh coat of paint and a full safety inspection. Roman remembered coming here almost every evening, hanging out with Wyatt after their high school classes, playing basketball in the driveway or Resident Evil on the PlayStation.

As they turned onto the familiar street, Roman

was flooded with even more emotion. He wondered if Wyatt held on to the same memories, with the same golden glow around the edges. Or were his memories veiled in trauma and pain, covered by a curtain of red.

He wouldn't blame him, not at all.

That's when he spotted him. Wyatt, looking absolutely scared shitless as he was being tossed into the back of a black town car by two men—both of them wearing lion claw necklaces.

Roman's blood boiled, his entire body flushing with heat as the town car sped forward. Roman pulled his gun from the holster, not even needing to give Mustang a command. She slammed on the pedal and launched them forward.

The driver of the town car spotted them, making a sudden left and accelerating in an effort to race ahead.

This checkup had *not* just turned into a full-blown car chase.

"Don't lose them," Roman said as they bounced off the curb, turning onto a dirt road that cut through someone's backyard. The town car tore through the fence, a wooden stake flying past Roman's head as he leaned out the window, gun raised and heart slamming against his ribs. He didn't have a clear shot, the tints on the car an impenetrable black.

"Get me next to them," he shouted at Mustang over the roaring wind.

"Hold on to your dicks, boys." She reached for the red switch on the dash and flipped it. The car turned into a rocket, the acceleration forcing Roman back into his seat and rattling his skull.

I'm coming for you, Wyatt. I won't let you get hurt again. Ever.

Chapter 5

Wyatt Hernandez

WYATT HAD NEVER FELT this kind of raw and unfiltered fear before. His shoulders were shaking uncontrollably as he was shoved into the back of a car, falling facedown with his hands tied behind his back. He rolled onto the car's floor as they sped forward, the men shouting commands around him as they raced ahead. Wyatt tried getting up but was thrown back down as they made a sharp turn, slamming his forehead against the driver's seat.

The sharp pain brought with it dark black stars that twinkled around the edges of Wyatt's vision. He gripped onto his consciousness with everything he had, knowing that passing out now would likely be a massive mistake.

"Where are you taking me?" he cried out from the floor.

His answer was a kick to the ribs. "That car is

gaining on us," the man said, ignoring a whimpering Wyatt and cocking his gun.

Car? Someone's chasing us?

A distant spark of hope lit up in his chest. Was someone trying to rescue him?

Was it Roman?

Wyatt used all his core strength to wiggle his way up onto his knees, leaning against the car seat as they took another turn. A loud metallic clang rang through the car, and Wyatt watched as pieces of fence flew past the windows. The car gained some air, jumping over a speed bump and slamming back down on the other side, Wyatt bouncing like a rag doll.

He just had to keep calm. He could make it out of this, as bleak as it seemed. If it was really Roman that was chasing after them, then these kidnappers were in for a really rough time. When Roman wanted something, he turned into a saltwater crocodile clamping its jaws around his prey's neck. Wyatt remembered liking that about him the most, how intensely passionate and driven he'd become when he wanted something. It turned into a double-edged sword that ended up stabbing Wyatt directly through the chest, but maybe this time, the sword would be aimed at the kidnappers instead.

"I've got a shot on the leader," one of the men said, the one closest to Wyatt. He leaned against the back seat, one eye shut and the other open as he took aim.

It is Roman.

Wyatt could see his savior (second time today, what the hell were the odds of that) in the passenger seat of the car tailing them, picking up a burst of sudden speed.

"Take it!" the driver shouted, spotting Roman's car gaining on them.

It would be a bullseye. Wyatt had no doubt about it. Roman was too close—even Wyatt could make that shot, his forehead forming a bright red bullseye. The man's finger pressed on the trigger at the exact moment Wyatt's teeth sunk into the back of his leg.

The man gave a screech and pulled the trigger, an ear-splitting bang filling the car as glass rained down on the white leather seats.

He had missed his shot and was turning that rage onto the reason: Wyatt.

"You fucking little bitch." He grabbed Wyatt by the collar and threw him against the car door.

"Mauricio, focus! Take another shot."

"Oh, I will." Mauricio brought his gun and pressed it up against Wyatt's throat. "I think you made me bleed, motherfucker."

"Shoot, shoot!"

Wyatt shut his eyes, bracing for the end. Would it hurt? Would he feel anything at all, or would it all just switch to black? His cheeks were wet from tears he hadn't realized were falling. His shoulders had stopped shaking, the fear becoming so strong, so potent, that it had a paralytic effect on him.

Another gunshot. More glass. More bangs. The car jerked to the left, and someone shouted, "He's dead!" before one last blast of a gun. A warm spray of blood went across Wyatt's neck. The car swerved, and he was thrown to the floor again, eyes still clamped shut. He said, "Please," over and over again. There wasn't any pain, but maybe that was the adrenaline hard at work.

The car bounced two more times before there was a loud crash, and the car came to a complete stop, Wyatt hitting his shoulder against the center console, a heavy body falling on top of him and pinning him down. He tried pushing him off but was lodged underneath the weight, and the smoke that began to fill the car's interior only made this situation catastrophically worse.

The door opened, and the body on top of him was yanked off. Wyatt looked up and into Roman's eyes, hand outstretched and reaching under Wyatt. "Come on, this thing's about to blow."

Wyatt didn't need any more urging. He crawled out of the car and was helped onto his feet by Roman. They ran from the flames that started to rise from the front of the car, the hood resembling a metallic accordion pressed into a leaning palm tree. Seconds later, the flames reached the gas tank, the explosion consuming the entire car and nearly knocking Wyatt over, heat smacking against the back of his neck.

"Are you okay? Are you hurt anywhere?"

Roman held on to Wyatt's elbows, clear concern reflecting back at Wyatt. He shook his head. "I'm not hurt. I'm fine. I'm fine." He took a deep breath, feeling very far from fine. His brain swam with questions, the shock making it hard to string together coherent sentences.

"Roman, we have to go."

Wyatt looked to the curly-haired girl sitting behind the driver's seat of a bright pink Audi. A couple of bullets had torn through the mirror, leaving behind some wires attached to a piece of glass. The other car was completely engulfed in flames now, none of the men who had abducted him making it out.

"I know I have a lot of explaining to do," Roman said, hands still around Wyatt's elbows. "But I need you to come with us."

A part of this whole ordeal felt familiar, an unruly and unpredictable kind of chaos that Roman had always brought into Wyatt's life. Trouble always seemed to follow the green-eyed daredevil, and for a while, Wyatt had found it entertaining. It was a way to escape the doldrums of his life, kind of like how his free ride to Yale and guaranteed gig at Google would have done. He had the ticket to a better life but had to give it all up because of the very man that was standing in front of him. And what had Roman given up?

Nothing. Roman wasn't the kind of guy to give anything up, not his time or his money or his heart.

"And what about my sister? I need to make sure she's okay." Wyatt felt a fresh wave of panic wash over him.

"Julie's going to be fine. The Pride is after you; they aren't the type to go for the family connections. But just to make sure, I'll have someone keep an eye on her. And you can call her on the way to our hideout."

Wyatt took a deep breath, feeling as if the world was spinning at double the regular speed. He expected to be launched off the ground and into the sky at any moment. Nothing felt real, and yet he had no doubt that it was.

"This is insane," Wyatt said, shoulders beginning to tremble.

"I know. It's crazy and insane and fucking batshit, but you have to trust me, Wyatt. Come with me. I'll keep you safe. The Pride is after you, and they aren't going to stop hunting you until they've got you."

"But why? What the hell do they want with me?"

Police sirens sounded in the distance, no doubt drawn by the huge column of dark smoke that billowed into the air. They were in the industrial part of town, a row of empty warehouses locked up for the weekend, graffiti creating a colorful mosaic backdrop against the burning car. "I'll explain everything later, but we have to go. Now."

Wyatt was once again paralyzed, though not by fear this time but by indecision. He could say "fuck this" and walk away, wait for the police to arrive so he could give his account, and get the hell home. He didn't need to get dragged into Roman Ashford's bullshit, not again.

Except... it sounded to Wyatt as if he was already involved. These men had clearly wanted him for something, and if Roman was right, then going home would only be putting his sister in danger again. He couldn't have that. Even if that meant getting into the car with a man who had ruined his life once before and saved it twice after.

Wyatt shook his head, pulling his arms back from Roman's grip. "Alright. Let's go."

Deep down, somewhere past the roiling panic and increasing dread that nestled in his gut, down past the marrow in his bones and the cells in his blood, Wyatt knew that he would regret this decision, knew it without the shadow of a doubt.

He got in the car anyway.

Chapter 6

Roman Ashford

No one inside the car spoke a word as Mustang wove through some light traffic, driving over a long bridge that looked out to the bay, the setting sun reflected back in a shifting canvas of oranges and blues and purples. Roman stole the occasional glance at the rearview mirror, looking at Wyatt and trying to read the thoughts that swirled behind those honey-brown eyes. He used to be an expert at reading Wyatt, able to easily tell the difference between his hangry glares and his exhausted looks.

Time changed that, just like it had changed Wyatt. He was more filled in, the skinny little computer nerd Roman had come to know turned into a bulkier twunk of a man, a five-o'clock shadow growing on his normally shaved face. He no longer wore his hair long and instead had it buzzed down, and his glasses had been traded in for a pair of contacts. Roman wanted to tell him that he looked good, that he missed him, that he was sorry for ever fucking up his life, that every single night he dreamed of a different outcome between them.

Roman didn't say shit. The silence in the car grew heavier, broken only by Phantom clearing his throat and Mustang humming a song.

The sun had set completely by the time they reached their hideout. Wyatt looked out the window and spoke for the first time since getting in the car. "Uh, why the hell are we at the aquarium?"

Mustang reached a locked gate, a curving blue sign above it reading Miami Aquarium. She pressed a button on the dash, and the gate started to swing open.

"Because we're feeding you to the sharks, buddy." Phantom reached over and gave Wyatt a friendly squeeze, which Wyatt didn't seem to appreciate, judging by the twist in his brows.

"Because we're home," Roman clarified, even though Wyatt still had a thousand questions written all over his face.

Mustang drove them through an empty parking lot and down a narrow road, wrapping around the back of a few administrative buildings and bringing them into a covered garage. Three other brightly colored sports cars were parked inside, all of them Mustang's babies. She pulled into the spot between

The Sunset Job

the corvette and the BMW, clapping her hands and saying, "You have arrived," in a near-exact imitation of the GPS voice.

"You live at the aquarium?" Wyatt asked as he got out of the car.

"Not all the time," Roman answered, leading the way through a door and into a brightly lit hallway.

"I do," Phantom said.

"Same," Mustang echoed. "I think it's better than paying some scummy landlord or making the bank's pockets fatter. Here, I don't have rent, and I can go hang out with the dolphins whenever I want. Pretty fucking sweet."

"But... how? Where do you guys sleep?"

"We've got rooms," Phantom said. "Thanks to our fearless leader. Right, Roman?"

Wyatt looked to Roman, eyes narrowing, plump lips turning into a pout. Even the harsh fluorescent lighting couldn't take away from how attractive Wyatt was, reigniting a flame inside Roman's cobweb-infested chest, flooding him with memories of their time together. Nights he'd never forget, nights he had spent wishing he had it all back.

"The owner owes me a massive favor," Roman explained. "I convinced him to let us remodel an old sea lion enclosure. He agreed, gave us full access to the aquarium, and told all the employees to look the other way." He didn't want to explain to Wyatt exactly *why* the owner of the aquarium owed him so much since it involved someone getting mauled by a tiger shark and Roman robbing two hundred thousand dollars' worth of rare jewels. Wyatt already looked like he was three seconds away from bolting, which was the last thing Roman wanted.

"I'm still so confused," Wyatt said, hand rubbing his face.

Roman stopped at a set of double doors, hips pressing against the bumper. He wore an easy, cocky smirk that appeared to annoy Wyatt, whose eyes narrowed to tiny slits. "Don't worry, I'll clear everything up tonight. But first, welcome."

Roman threw open the door, causing Wyatt's jaw to drop, his eyes no longer narrow slits but instead nearly bulging from his skull.

"Holy shit," he said, stepping into the domed space, lights twinkling all around the concrete ceiling as if a permanent constellation had been pulled down from the night sky and installed into the space. The dark wood floors, freshly polished, complemented the deep burgundies and dashing blues of the eclectic furniture, the room feeling like it belonged in a designer penthouse somewhere in central London. A massive mural of a blue whale swimming through a rainbow stretched from floor to ceiling, framing a large window that looked into a tank full of tropical fish.

"This is the common room," Roman said, smiling as he admired the room. They had finished it only

The Sunset Job

last month, but he was happy with how lived-in it already felt. Bang Bang had a collection of sneakers by the door, and Mustang had her favorite beanbag chair close to the flat-screen TV, where a treasure trove of video game consoles was connected. The kitchen was full of Phantom's favorite aloe vera drinks, and the hall that led to the bedrooms was covered in surreal watercolor landscape art by none other than Rose "Doc" Lee, the crew's on-call healer and mender.

Roman pointed toward a small kitchen facing out to the big-screen TV. "Usually, Bang Bang cooks us dinner, but sometimes, I like to surprise everyone."

"Yeah, with a sudden bout of food poisoning," Mustang said under her breath, earning an eye roll from Roman and an enthusiastic nod from Phantom.

"Roman was always a disaster in the kitchen," Wyatt quipped. It surprised Roman, the casual link back to their past. It surprised him, and it thrilled him. What else was Wyatt holding on to? Yes, having him here was very much a necessity if he wanted the heist to go off smoothly, but it wasn't the only reason why Roman was happy to have his saltshaker back in his orbit.

"Come," Roman said. "Let me show you the bedrooms."

From somewhere outside, a playful bunch of seals called out into the night. Roman always enjoyed the sounds of the aquarium after hours, when the giggling kids and semi-drunk parents were out of the picture. If he listened closely, he could hear the clicks and chirps from the pilot whales that were nearby.

There were five bedrooms, none of them very large but big enough considering no one paid to live there. Each one had a twin-size bed pushed up against the wall, with a wardrobe and small workstation that was being used as a dirty-laundry collector by Bang Bang. The bathrooms were dorm-style except for the showers, which Roman made sure were as bougie as possible, with rainfall showerheads and massaging jets that came out of the wall.

If he wanted a good crew, he knew he had to make them as comfortable as possible.

Plus, Roman really loved a good shower.

"This is incredible," Wyatt said as they found their way back into the main room. "I'm still not sure if this is all a dream." His eyes flicked to Roman's, a spark lighting up in his gut before Wyatt looked away. "Or a nightmare."

"It's neither," Roman assured him.

"Roman, I still don't even know what I'm doing here. I don't know why a criminal organization is after me, and I don't know why you showed up in my life after years of being gone."

"I hate that it's been years, and I hate what I did to you, Wyatt. I regret it. Every single day of my life, I wish I could turn back time and make it right by

The Sunset Job

you. You should have been the one staying at Yale, and I should have been the one kicked out."

"It's not even just about getting kicked out, Roman. I almost went to jail. I almost lost everything. My sister would be out on the streets right now if I wasn't around, if I had ended up on Rikers for the rest of my life. I still have full-blown fucking night terrors about that time. Sometimes I wake up crying, thinking that my bedroom is a jail cell."

Roman felt his heart start to crack around the edges. Years of being in his business meant a hardening of his emotions, built through the scar tissue that comes from getting backstabbed and used. That callous shell grew around him, encasing him and distancing him from the emotional soul he used to have.

But one puppy-dog-eyed look from Wyatt ripped away at the protective layer. "I'm sorry, Wyatt. I wish I could offer more than words right now, but if those aren't enough, then I can promise you that once this job is done, you and your sister will have everything you've ever dreamed of and more."

"What is it, then? Why am I here, Roman?"

Roman could spot a slight tremble in Wyatt's shoulders as he looked around. He was right. Roman had kept him in the dark for long enough. It was time to lay it all out on the table. Wyatt deserved at least that much. Even though Roman liked to keep as many cards close to his chest as he could, he knew that in this instance, being as open with his crew as possible would lead to the best results.

"Alright," he said, turning to Mustang, who was munching on a pickle straight out of the jar. "Get the group together. We're having a meeting."

Chapter 7

Wyatt Hernandez

WYATT SAT on the edge of the couch, perched like a rare bird ready to take flight at the slightest provocation. It had only taken fifteen minutes for Roman to gather his crew, the room filling with friendly banter and relaxed laughter. It was clear to Wyatt that this team had chemistry, but what the hell was Roman using them for? He'd always been into some black-hat kind of tactics—hence the immense rift between them, Wyatt preferring to stay on the right side of the law—but had he turned his passion for shady shit into a full-on professional crime ring?

"Here, drink this." It was the girl they called Mustang. Monica was her real name, but Wyatt could see where her nickname had been derived from, his neck still sore from the whiplash with some of her turns.

"What is it?"

"Vodka."

Wyatt lifted up the full glass, eyes wide.

"Joking. It's water. Although you might wish it was vodka by the end of all this."

She went over to plop down on her beanbag, whipping out her phone and scrolling with the same speed she drove with. Wyatt took a gulp of the cool water, sitting back down and observing the gathered group, all of them different but effortlessly blending together.

"Where's Mimic?" the big burly one asked. Bang Bang was his name. Wyatt remembered him from the science museum, when he came in with his golden pistol and nearly shot a man's head off. Under normal circumstances, Wyatt would be working to get as far away from him as possible, never a fan of guns or those who enjoyed them as much as Bang Bang seemed to.

But nothing about this was normal. Nothing.

"She should be here soon," Roman said, leaning on the back of a green velvet armchair. Wyatt didn't want to think about how attractive he looked, wearing a black V-neck shirt that dipped down a muscular chest, highlighted by four silver necklaces, one of them appearing like thick chain links that wrapped right around his neck. He tried not to think about how good Roman looked in the dark jeans that shaped themselves around his meaty thighs. He definitely didn't want to think about all those nights he had spent getting lost in those crystal-green eyes, hands trailing up and down that muscular body, tender kisses morphing into hungry moans.

But of course, that was *all* Wyatt could think about.

"Let's get started without her. She already knows this first part, anyway." Roman went over to the light switch and flicked it off. He pulled a remote from his pocket, and the wall was filled with an image of the science museum.

"So this is where the job started and also where it went balls-up to the sky. We fucked up thinking that the Pride wouldn't be there. Thankfully, we still managed to make it out. Now, as for the *why* we were there." He clicked a button, and the image changed, showing a brochure for the *Writing Through the Ages* exhibit, depicting the dozens of different and ancient texts the museum had acquired, from pavement illustrations and leading all the way up to a holographic poem written to appear as if in stars. One of the first-ever periodic tables was included, as well as one of Darwin's original works. Wyatt had been excited about it, especially since his manager had brought him in on creating a special VR experience for the kids to try.

But what the hell did Roman want with any of that?

He clicked the button, and the image faded into

that of a leather-bound book, its cover etched with a tree that had roots that wrapped around the spine and reached the back of the book. The pages were brushed with gold, and the title was scrawled in a fragile hand: *The Tome of Tomorrow*.

"This is what we're after," Roman said, eyes scanning over the assembled crew. "This book, written by an eccentric man named Remy Torrent, is said to actually contain accurate predictions of the future. The economic crash of the early 2000s is in there, along with two accurate earthquake predictions and a nearly exact dollar-value prediction of the price of Bitcoin when it had reached its peak just last year."

Bang Bang cleared his throat and pointed toward the door. Wyatt was surprised to see a face he recognized.

"Mimic, everything good?" Roman asked as the woman—same one who had been wearing a wig at the museum—walked over and sat down on the beanbag, taking off her leather jacket and folding it in her lap.

"Not exactly. The museum is closing for a few weeks, and the exhibit is moving. It'll either be in New York or LA, they haven't decided yet."

"That's fine," Roman said. "The book isn't the only thing we need. There's two more pieces of this puzzle that need to fall in place before we're all filthy rich. One of those pieces is here." The image on the wall shifted, showing a towering castle framed by a mountain range, a row of palm trees marking the long drive down to the spiraling iron gates, and two golden lions flanking either side of the entrance.

"This is Castillo de Dragón Gris, or Grey Drake castle, located an hour's drive away from Madrid, and it's where we're heading to next."

Wyatt's eyebrows jerked up his forehead. Spain? He'd never even been out of the state, much less out of the country. What the hell had he gotten himself into?

"Grey Drake castle is home to the Flors, a family who's clung to their royal heritage like a starved rat clinging to the only sliver of cheese it's got left. The daughter, Beatriz Flor, is having a sixteenth birthday party this weekend, and it won't only be her friends in attendance. Giovanni Gorga will also be there." Roman clicked the remote, and a handsome man's face filled the wall. "He's our target. An influential real estate developer and multi-millionaire, as well as Remy's longtime lover. Normally, he's on his private island surrounded by a dozen different security measures, considering that he suffers from intense paranoia, which appeared to have struck him only after he became one of the world's wealthiest men."

"What's he got?" Bang Bang asked, popping a bright pink bubble between his lips.

"He's got a page from the *Tome of Tomorrow*.

Before Remy died—an aggressive type of bone cancer—he tore out two pages of his book and gave them to the two people he cared most about in this world: his lover and his mother. The book is worthless without those two pages. There are two phrases that, when said to the page holders, should cause them to give them up."

Mustang leaned over and grabbed Mimic's hand, massaging it while she asked her question. "What's on them?"

"You'll find out when we get them in hand."

Wyatt nearly rolled his eyes but shut them and dropped his head instead. Roman was always one to keep important details to himself, his level of trust in others as shallow as a puddle of dog piss on a New York City sidewalk.

"Mimic is supplying us with our identifications and disguises for the party," Roman continued. "Bang Bang and Phantom, you two are going in with the caterers. Mustang, you'll be driving the food truck. I'll be going in with Mimic as a married couple, while Wyatt and Doc stay behind and monitor cams. There will be two clear windows of opportunity—when the performance begins and everyone's distracted or when Giovanni steps away to take his daily call with his financial advisor, which he will no doubt try to do. It's in those moments that we'll have to grab the page."

"Sounds pretty easy," Phantom said, taking a swig of beer.

"It always does," Mustang shot back. "And it never is."

"Truth." Phantom chugged the rest of his beer, the can clinking against the table as he set it down.

"After we get the page from Giovanni, we then have to pay a visit to Remy's mother: Amelie LaFleur, a famous Parisian baker who lives and works just streets away from the Louvre. Her son left her a huge fortune before his death and warned her of the potential for treasure hunters like us coming for the page, so it won't be as easy as waiting until she's out of the house to break in and snatch it."

"And why is this book, these pages, why are they so valuable?" Wyatt asked, the words feeling weird coming out of his mouth. He had felt like a visitor, an observer. Someone sitting in the audience as the curtain is drawn up and the actors hit their marks. Having a voice, asking questions, it took him out of the audience and placed him directly on the center of the stage.

Roman didn't answer immediately. Even though the room was dark, Wyatt could see him weighing out different answers, trying to parse which slivers of information he could give out and which ones he needed to hold back.

"Remy was a fan of puzzles," Roman said. "Not only was he a technical savant and a Nostradamuslite, but he also liked to play games, and still does even after death. He specifically tore out those two pages because with them in hand, the book turns into a key, and with that key, we can unlock all of our wildest dreams."

Wyatt couldn't hold back the eye roll this time. More vague answers and runarounds, talking about dreams and keys when he should really be talking about specifics.

"And why am I being dragged along?" Wyatt asked, determined to get a solid answer.

"Because once we have all the pieces of the puzzle, that's when the final roadblock appears. We'll need you to hack through a virtual vault, using the information we gathered along the way to help you get in. Once you're in, we'll have reached the pot of infinite gold. We'll all be rich, beyond our wildest imagination."

That earned a loud cheer from Mustang and a hoot-hoot from Bang Bang, Phantom dancing his empty beer can across the table. Wyatt couldn't deny he felt the same kind of excitement spark in his chest, even though it was quickly overshadowed by the doubt and fear still multiplying inside him. Roman wasn't saying everything—that part was clear, and it made him nervous. It didn't help that the last time he had worked with Roman, he'd got himself expelled from college and nearly jailed for doing exactly what Roman was asking him to do now. He had given up his black-hat-hacking life after nearly losing everything, and yet here he was, reaching for the same black hat.

But if it meant never having to worry about money again... the things he could do. His sister had always wanted to go to Disney World, and from the way Roman was speaking, Wyatt started to think he'd be able to buy Disney by the time this was all over. Sure, he'd have to work alongside the annoyingly cocky (and devastatingly fucking handsome, ugh) Roman, but as long as he kept him an arm's length away at all times, then Wyatt figured he'd be fine.

"Any more questions?" Roman said, moving toward the light switch.

"When do we start?" Mustang asked.

"Our flight to Spain leaves tomorrow."

Bang Bang got up, nearly knocking over his chair. "Ah, shit, I have to pack. Think we'll have time to spend at a beach?."

Roman laughed, raising the remote. "Yes, we'll have a free night. But wait, before you leave to go pack your lube and Speedos, I wanted to finish with one more thing. I know the majority of us have been working together for some time now, and through all that time, we've gone through some shit, but we've always done it without a banner. That changes tonight, because I'm officially welcoming you all to..."

The image changed, creating a bright white backdrop that highlighted the rainbow already painted on the wall. Letters began appearing, as if drawn by an invisible hand, following the curve of the mural, spelling out the words that Wyatt would always remember:

Rainbow's Seven.

Chapter 8

Wyatt Hernandez

R*AINBOW'S* S*EVEN*.

The name rolled around in Wyatt's thoughts as he set his backpack down next to the neatly made bed, the white linen sheets looking extra comfortable after the intense day that had unfurled behind him. He found a semblance of comfort in knowing the plan and meeting the others involved, although he still didn't have the full picture, Roman clearly holding things back for reasons only he knew. This was when the trust factored into the equation, except Wyatt didn't have all that much trust to begin with. Roman had screwed him over once before, and there was no guarantee that it wouldn't happen again.

That scared him... but not enough to call it quits. The stakes were too high, the reward too grand. Wyatt had to see this through, and he'd have to keep his guard up the entire time.

He looked around the narrow room he'd been given, a circular window above the bed letting in some of the bright moonlight that filtered down from a cloudless sky. The lamp on the desk was on, Wyatt's laptop open to a Google search on the *Tome of Tomorrow*.

Mustang had driven him back home so he could grab some things and say bye to his sister, which ended up being more emotional than he had expected. He tearfully promised her that he'd be okay and back home in a couple of weeks and let her know that she'd be protected the entire time. He told her to stay with an aunt and uncle on their cattle farm in central Florida, the closest familial ties they had. He was confident that she'd be safe there, regardless of how it all turned out. The drive back to the aquarium had Wyatt fighting back tears, filled with doubt and questions. Had he just lied to his sister? Was he making a mistake by agreeing to all this?

He sat down at the desk and clicked through the pages of terribly made websites that seemed more concerned with pop-ups asking for his email address than sharing any valuable information on the book. Wyatt had heard of it when the exhibit was first scheduled at the museum, but no one ever alluded to how valuable it really was. Wyatt wondered if the curators at the museum even knew, and if they didn't, then how the hell had Roman figured it out?

The Sunset Job

In the midst of all the hows and whats, Wyatt was sure of one thing: he wasn't coming up with any answers that night. A body-shaking yawn took over as he shut the laptop. With an exhausted sigh, he dropped his head in his arm cave and shut his eyes, his batteries drained down to empty. He figured he should get at least a few hours of sleep before boarding a plane and flying across the country.

How the hell did this happen to me?

He kicked off his shoes, pulled off his socks, and was working on his pants when a knock on the door made him freeze mid-thigh. He pulled them back on and went for the door, opening it to see a smiling Bruno 'Bang Bang' offering him a dew-covered bottle of beer.

"I think you need this," he said, letting himself in and handing the beer over. Wyatt blinked a couple of times and gave a fuck-it shrug before taking a chug of the bubbly golden drink. Bang Bang was right—he definitely needed this.

"How you holding up?" Bang Bang asked, sitting down on the edge of the bed. His massive size made it seem like furniture belonging inside of a dollhouse. Wyatt was normally intimidated (and slightly turned on) by bigger, stronger, testosterone-filled men, the ones who could either be fight-thirsty bullies or gentle gay giants, depending.

It seemed like Bang Bang was more of the latter, and that was something Wyatt could appreciate.

"I'm alright," Wyatt said, taking another swig. "It's a lot to take in."

"Funny, I tend to hear that a lot." He gave a cocky wink, and Wyatt rolled his eyes, both of them laughing while a crack formed in the ice between them.

"So, how do you know Roman?" Bang Bang asked. His big blue eyes glittered under a direct beam of moonlight, competing with the golden crosses that dangled from either ear. "Feels like you two had a past."

"Things were messy." Wyatt wasn't sure if he wanted to keep going, but Bang Bang pulled off an impressive puppy-eyed look for someone who resembled a full-grown bulldog. The words fell out without any more coaxing. "We knew each other when we were kids, grew up only a few blocks from each other. We were best friends, always had each other's backs, even when that meant both of us getting in trouble even when it should have been just one. We spent nearly every day together, and at some point during our senior year of high school, things took a more physical turn. We both got accepted to our dream college, Yale, and I felt like nothing could take away my happiness. I thought I'd ride that ecstasy all the way to the finish line.

"I was such a fucking idiot. Everything came tumbling down a year later when Roman convinced me to hack into the grading system and change his grade so that he could keep his scholarship. I did it, and I got caught, and everything else after that somehow got worse and worse. It was like a domino effect of life-altering fuckery, all kicked off by Mr. Rainbow's Seven himself."

"Yeah, you're right, that does sound messy, *broki*. But here's to new beginnings, eh?" He lifted his glass and offered an infectious smile, which surprised Wyatt when his lips curled to mirror Bang Bangs. He clinked their glasses together and drank.

"I don't know if I'll ever have a new beginning with Roman. I'm here because I want a better life for me and my sister, and that's it. When it's over, it'll be over between Roman and me, too. I've already been burned once, and it ain't happening again."

Bang Bang arched a bushy brow, crossing a tattooed arm across his chest and scratching at the side of his neck. It was an impressive tattoo, the entire sleeve on display since he was wearing a tank top. There were light blue peonies and dark red roses flowing gracefully up his forearm, wrapping around the main event: a pin-up tattoo of a man with a pair of booty shorts bulging with the thickness of the thighs, one leg kicked back and one arm holding up a bright golden pistol, lips pressed with a smile against the barrel.

"What about you?" Wyatt asked. "How did you meet Roman, and what did he do to fuck up your life?"

Bang Bang gave a deep belly laugh at that before finishing off his bear and wiping his lips with the back of his hand. "Roman and I met at a bathhouse, actually."

"Of course you did," Wyatt said.

"We were there working the same job. There was a meeting being held there between the heads of two rival gangs. This was up in New York, and I had been hired to take one out while Roman was there for the other. Big payday for the both of us, but shit went south. I got shot in the leg, and Roman got a knife slash across the chest, both of us fighting while butt-ass naked, but we made it out together, and we were both successful. Figured we should work together after that. Have been ever since."

"What a feel-good story," Wyatt responded with a sarcastic edge in his smile. "And I assume it's all just been guns and roses since?"

"Why don't you ask him?" Bang Bang said, eyes drawing up and to the side toward the door that was now open. Roman filled the frame with his broad build, an easygoing smile playing on that perpetual baby face of his.

"Hey, boys, mind if I join?"

Chapter 9

Roman Ashford

Roman couldn't sleep. He thought crashing at the aquarium would be a good idea but now started to wonder if maybe his condo would have been better. His entire body buzzed with a current that kept his eyes open and heart racing. It wasn't nerves or fear or apprehension but excitement. Roman could see the finish line now, and beyond that, he could see the prize. His entire life—and the lives of his entire crew—were about to be astronomically different. He just needed to get them across that finish line.

And then there was Wyatt, whose big brown eyes and rare-but-effortless grin were no longer confined to Roman's dreams anymore. He was back—his best friend, his awkward first time, his first love, his last devastating heartbreak. Roman had fucked around after their breakup but had never felt the same kind of "sunshine in the coffee cup" kind of feeling he used to describe to Wyatt.

And then Roman went and fucked it all up. He had derailed Wyatt's entire life, ruining his chance at a degree from his dream college and fucking up his shot at a dream job, and there was nothing Roman could have done except profusely apologize.

None of those apologies landed. Wyatt stopped answering any of his texts or calls, and the last eight years they had spent together as best friends (and two as boyfriends) were flushed unceremoniously down the drain. Roman lasted two years at Yale before he dropped out, his adventure-hungry and risk-seeking lifestyle leading him to find work with an uncle in Greece, a man who happened to be one of the most prolific grifters of the twenty-first century. Roman had learned a lot from his uncle, up until the day he was found dead in a lake with a bullet through the skull.

To this day, Roman still wasn't sure who killed his uncle. One of the things he vowed to do with the money from this job was to find the killer and make him pay for taking one of the last blood relatives Roman had left on this spinning rock. If everything went according to plan, then he'd have his revenge served on a gold-encrusted platter.

He got up from his bed, deciding it was time to take a trip to the kitchen for a beer. As he padded barefoot back to his room, he heard noise coming

The Sunset Job

from behind Wyatt's door, Bang Bang's voice carrying into the hall as if the guy was speaking through a megaphone.

He considered just continuing on his walk back to the room, drinking his beer as he went over the plans for tomorrow's heist. But it had been so long since he and Wyatt had talked...

He knocked on the door, opened it, and smiled at a surprised Wyatt. "Hey, boys, mind if I join?"

Bang Bang stood up, coming over and slapping a hand on Roman's shoulder. "I was just about to head out. Doc wanted to watch a movie with me tonight."

"I'm sure she did," Roman said, smirking at Bang Bang. He knew his best friend understood the risks that came with dating within the crew, which made it all the more surprising when he and Doc started getting close. Nothing official was announced between the two of them, but Roman didn't expect it to take much longer.

Bang Bang gave a bearlike growl meant to be a chuckle as he left, closing the door behind him. The room became suffocatingly silent. Roman blinked, shuffled a couple of feet, looked around at the bare white-bricked walls.

"Want to go for a walk?" Roman asked, deciding that a stroll under the stars was exactly what this moment called for.

"No, I think I'm good." Wyatt started to untie his

sneakers. Roman contained his surprise and cleared his throat before trying again.

"It's a nice night. I can show you around the aquarium."

"I'm fine."

Damn. That felt like a bucket of ice getting poured over Roman's head. Wyatt still had a strong hold to what had happened in the past, and he couldn't be blamed for that. Roman considered calling it a night and leaving him alone, but a spark of their old chemistry lit somewhere in his chest, bringing back that butterfly-field feeling he had nearly forgotten existed. He'd gotten so used to being icy-cold and distant, keeping lovers as far as he kept his enemies, none of them ever getting as close to him as Wyatt had.

And for good reason. Wyatt was incomparable, unmatchable. He stood on his own pedestal, with a smile that lured Roman in as if he'd been hooked on a fishing line. And not only was he attractive, but Wyatt was intelligent, too. One of the smartest people Roman had ever had in his life, and that list included Roman himself. He was quick-witted and stubborn and loved all the same jokes Roman did and made the perfect little spoon and had the perfect rock to his hips when he was rid—

Roman wasn't going back to his room just yet. He decided to take the blunt approach. "I'm going to try one more time: let's go for a walk around the dolphin deck and talk about all the shit that we need to talk about. Sound good?"

Wyatt arched a brow, chewed on his cheek. He was going to say no, Roman could see it in his eyes. Fuck. This wasn't how he wanted to start off the first leg of their heist.

"Fine, let's go." Wyatt got up, grabbing his drink. "I've always wanted a private aquarium tour anyway, and this is free. Usually that's about a thousand dollars... which is still cheaper than the parking."

Roman laughed as he followed Wyatt out of the room. "Do you usually have trouble sleeping the night before a big job?" Wyatt asked, looking down at the ground as they walked.

"Nah, I usually sleep like a baby."

"Really? Something different about this one, then?"

"Everything's different." Roman looked at Wyatt, a large part of him unable to believe this was real. That he could actually reach out and touch him.

Completely fucking wild.

They left the living space and walked out into the warm Miami night, a couple of thick clouds drifting slowly across a sky devoid of stars. There were lights that shone down on the path, illuminating signs that pointed toward the shark tunnel. Palm trees gently swayed in the breeze, the same breeze that carried over Wyatt's intoxicating scent. It reminded Roman of the nights he'd fall asleep with his nose buried in Wyatt's hair, the warmth from their naked bodies working better than any blanket ever could. An ember formed at the base of Roman's spine, flickering up and outward, the jockstrap he still wore feeling tighter. From somewhere in the distance, a couple of loud splashes and a sequence of barking sounds could be heard.

"That's Bert and Ernie, the sea lions. They like to stay up late and fuck around with everyone else trying to sleep."

Wyatt chuckled, looking around with a small grin on his face, as if he was working to hold back the rest of it. "So, are we really the only people here right now?"

"Nah, there are a couple of night keepers and security guards that walk around. They all know the deal, though. No questions are ever asked."

"That's pretty incredible, the way you managed to secure this."

Roman nodded, turning down a wide path and leading them toward a set of stairs that were underneath a massive set of shark teeth. "What about you? What incredible things have you been up to?"

Wyatt cocked his head. "You mean my award-winning work creating a five-minute VR experience for Tomes of Whatever that took me about a hundred hours of unpaid overtime to finish?"

"*Unpaid?*"

"Yes, unpaid. Although I may be exaggerating the hours."

"Well, I guarantee you this job is paid. And you won't have to worry about the museum ever again."

Wyatt scoffed. "And we all know Roman Ashford has a great track record with keeping his promises."

"Fair enough." Roman wanted to put his hands up and tell Wyatt to just throw the punch. Knock him across the jaw and get all the pent-up anger and frustration out.

And then after, he'd ask Wyatt to kiss it better. He'd grab his hands and wrap them around his waist, pulling Wyatt onto him as they reunited in more ways than one.

"Have you been working on any passion projects?" Roman asked, pulling his thoughts back on track, even though the rogue throb in his shorts made that difficult.

"A couple, yeah. I just haven't had any time to focus on them. I also feel like I'm behind, somehow. I had to teach myself everything from the ground up, and I couldn't even focus on anything until the last few—why am I even telling you any of this."

"Because I want to hear it," Roman said as they walked under the gaping shark jaw, entering the underwater tunnel. Immediately, they were surrounded by a school of gray and black fish, moving as if sharing one mind, their scales flashing under the lights.

"Really? Is that why you haven't called in the last, oh, I don't know, five years? "

"It's not—no..."

A thin thread of Roman's reactionary self wanted to snap back with the same question thrown back at Wyatt. Why hadn't he been the one to find Roman and reach out to him?

But Roman knew the answer to that question, and asking it now would only make things exponentially worse. So he swallowed his words and craned his neck, looking up as a hammerhead shark lazily swam past.

The two riled-up men slowly walked their way down the underwater tunnel in silence. A manta ray with a wingspan of at least four feet slowly drifted above them, appearing as if it were flying. Roman tried to think about the view, about the job, about the fucking weather. He tried to think of anything that wasn't pinning Wyatt up against the thick glass and kissing him the way he used to—without any restraints, devouring him whole and enjoying every second of it, every taste, every moan.

"I've missed you," Roman said, their walk slowing, the vulnerability in his own voice surprising him. "A lot."

"Why didn't you ever reach out, then? My number never changed."

"I don't have a good reason to offer you, Wyatt. I fucked up, and that fuckup ruined your life. That made me ashamed—it made me hurt for you and for what could have been. There was a time when I thought I was doing you a favor by staying away. You didn't need to get involved in the shit that was going on in my life." Roman rubbed the bridge of his nose. He hated apologizing, hated owning up to mistakes, and instead preferred to power through the turbulence and work to make the mistake right.

Tonight, he had to suck it up and let the words come without any conditions or subtext.

"I'm sorry. I should have stood up for you. I should have taken the fall—if not for you, then with you. I fucked up, and I'm sorry."

They stopped their walk, the entrance to the tunnel still a ways away. A wall of yellow and blue coral rose behind Wyatt, some clown fish drifting in and out of an anemone. It reminded Roman of a date they had been on, one of their first, when he had managed to somehow snag them a private behind-the-scenes tour and swimming session with the dolphins at this very aquarium. They were only seventeen, just having made things official between them, two starry-eyed queer kids living life as if every day were a fairy tale.

Fast-forward ten years and those starry-eyed boys no longer existed, replaced by hardened and skeptical men, scarred by the way their dreams shattered around them. The scar tissue throbbed with every one of Roman's heartbeats, reflected back at him through Wyatt's wide brown eyes.

"I know," Wyatt finally said after a moment of loaded silence. The blue hues of the surrounding water shifted across his face as he looked away from Roman. "You didn't force me to hack the school. No one was holding a gun to my head; no one made me do it. I may have been a little *coerced* to do it, but you didn't force me. But yes, you should have made things right somehow." He crossed his arms, turning his face back to Roman and pouting those puffy lips of his. A bolt of heat wedged itself in Roman's chest, spreading outward.

"I'm making things right with this job." Roman reached for Wyatt's hands. It was an instinct, buried somewhere deep underneath all the ice separating them. Wyatt didn't pull away, his hands closing around Roman's and feeling like a small piece of home. "You've got to trust me—I won't ever hurt you or betray you. I'm going to make it all up to you, alright?"

Wyatt sucked in a deep breath, eyes pinned to Roman's, searching for any signs of a lie. Roman wanted to kiss him, claim him all over again. He could practically taste Wyatt on his tongue, feel his body writhing and grinding. Roman's cock twitched against his thigh, swelling with need, his body reacting to the memories of their heat.

"We'll see," Wyatt said, pulling his hands back and slipping them into his pockets. He swallowed, his Adam's apple working as a target for Roman's lips. Would that make him angry, if Roman pushed in for a kiss? Or would it open up the floodgates?

Only one way to find out.

And Roman went in, completely shocked by the reaction he received.

Chapter 10

Wyatt Hernandez

AN ARM'S LENGTH AWAY. That's all Wyatt told himself he had to do to keep sane. He just needed to cosplay as Bubble Boy and separate himself from Roman at all times, making sure none of their body parts ever touched, none of their matches ever lit. It sounded easy, considering how much resentment and anger Wyatt still held on to, aimed directly at the man of the hour. He should have been able to sidestep Roman's kiss and tell him to fuck off. It would have kept things simpler, cleaner, easier.

Except the only step Wyatt made was forward, accepting the kiss and instantly being thrown back to when they were together, blindly in love and passionately expressing it. There'd be hours of play between them, sending Wyatt to Mars and back, blowing his brain each and every time. Wyatt hadn't been able to find that kind of chemistry again, not that he'd been working hard to look for it in the first place.

Still, the reminder of it was enough to pop whatever flimsy bubble Wyatt had tried to form around himself. The anger was still there, no doubt about that, but it now coiled itself like a waiting viper, ready to lash out once the flames of passion died down.

"Fuck," Roman said against Wyatt's lips, his body like a solid column of muscle against Wyatt's. "I've *really* missed this." He smiled into another kiss. Wyatt felt the exact same, but he wasn't about to say it out loud, answering instead by grabbing Roman's head and steering so that his tongue slipped deeper, swirling around Roman's. It was a taste he remembered clearly, indescribable and yet addictive all the same.

With their hips pushing against each other, grinding to the invisible beat of their kiss, it was easy for Wyatt to feel how turned on Roman was by this, and that drove him wild. His cock stiffened to match Roman's, both of their shorts doing a terrible job at holding back how excited they both were.

Wyatt reached down and stroked Roman's length, feeling it pulse from underneath the soft fabric. He licked his lips, still wet with Roman's kiss. "This is crazy."

"Things are going to get crazier, Wyatt. This job isn't going to be easy. The Pride is going to try to fuck us up at every step of the way, so let's make sure we enjoy tonight."

Roman had his hands down Wyatt's shorts, fingers sliding between his ass. Wyatt let his head fall back against the thick glass, looking up just as two manta rays drifted past. This had to be some kind of twisted dream. Wyatt was a fan of logic, and that really seemed to be the only logical explanation available to him. Either that or a gas leak that had him passed out in his bedroom.

"God, it feels so good to have you in my hands again." Roman nipped at Wyatt's neck as he spoke, Wyatt's eyes rolling back as a wave of pleasure crashed over him. He pushed back on Roman's hand, moaning when Roman's finger rubbed over his hole.

"We shouldn't—"

"We *should*. This is what you and I were made to do. To worship each other." His tongue traced a line up Wyatt's neck, flicking across his earlobe, his husky breath caressing the side of Wyatt's face and sending a tremble down to his knees. Every warning sign was going off; every single flashing red light was bright and angry, telling him to stop immediately. Roman had ruined his life once before and was only *just* beginning to apologize for it. He didn't deserve to be kissing Wyatt, to be holding and squeezing and pressing and stroking and—

"There aren't any cameras in here, right?" Wyatt

asked, shooting a glance toward either end of the curving tunnel, no sign of anyone in sight.

"None," Roman answered with a hungry grin, his hands moving from the back to the front, one hand closing around Wyatt's stiff cock and the other working on pulling down his shorts.

"Bert, the security guard, does walk around every hour, though," Roman said as Wyatt's shorts dropped to his ankles.

"Guess we should make this quick, then." Wyatt grabbed the base of his hard length and squeezed, a clear drop of precome pooling at the tip.

"Unfortunately," Roman said, licking his lips as he went down to his knees and leaned in. He took Wyatt into his mouth without using his hands, pressing them against the glass on either side of Wyatt instead. The wet, hot heat was nearly overwhelming as he watched Roman swallow him whole, as if he'd been starving for this. He took Wyatt down to the base, his nose buried in a well-trimmed, dark patch of hair, Wyatt's eyes rolling back in his head and a chesty moan being coaxed from his throat.

"Fuck, you taste so good, Wyatt." Roman licked up and down, swirling his tongue and lapping up whatever precome leaked from Wyatt's rock-hard dick. He started to push his hips forward, pushing his cock deeper down Roman's throat. He happily swallowed it, hands moving to grip Wyatt's thighs now, fingers kneading into the tensing muscle. Roman's erection tented his shorts, throbbing for attention. Wyatt wanted to give it but couldn't muster the words or strength to swap, his entire body melting into the soft and fluid motion of Roman blowing him.

"Jerk yourself off," Wyatt said, his eyes locked on the massive bulge, Roman's white shorts turning dark gray around the dripping tip. Roman didn't waste a second, pulling his cock out and stroking the impressive length, thick and hard as concrete, the blue lights of the water making it seem like they were under an Instagram filter.

Wyatt nearly started to drool.

"I'm getting close," he said, feeling his muscles tighten, the edge racing toward him with every one of Roman's needy slurps. And he wasn't just using his mouth, either, using his free hand to tug on Wyatt's tightening balls, a finger slipping back and pressing down, making Wyatt's toes curl down into his sneakers.

"Blow," Roman said, his lips glistening as he jerked Wyatt off. "Do it, Wyatt, give it to me."

Wyatt couldn't hold back if he wanted to. He cried out, the sound taking on an echo through the tunnel. Roman took him in his mouth and swallowed every last shot, a smile on his face as he jerked himself off harder, his balls unloading onto the floor in heavy ropes, his mouth still full of Wyatt's cock.

Wyatt smiled, his body flushed with a euphoria that he hadn't felt in ages.

The Sunset Job

Roman got back up on his feet, rubbing off the dirt from his knees and the come from his lips. He smiled, too, and that melted any last bits of ice that might have separated them. Wyatt giggled, like a little fucking schoolkid, his body flooded with endorphins and his brain having gone completely haywire. It was back to being freshmen in college, forgetting about things like classes and clubs and friends, instead spending hours and hours together in their dorms, a tangle of legs and arms and dick, sweaty and passionate and carefree.

It wasn't just the sex Wyatt was fondly remembering. It was also the hours they spent talking, about anything and everything. Roman had a way of making anything a conversation, and Wyatt enjoyed riding those trains of thought until the wheels didn't spin anymore. He also had a way of making Wyatt feel comfortable, at ease. As if nothing in the world could ever go wrong.

That's exactly what he was feeling as Roman put an arm around his waist, pulling him in again. "I'm going to make it all up to you, Wyatt. I promise. Let's just get to the end of this job together."

Wyatt felt a moment of post-nut clarity settle in. He stiffened, the sensation of being home flickering like the light of a dimming candle. "This won't be like the last time we worked together, right?"

"It won't. I swear it won't. I've grown. I've—shit's happened. It's changed me." There was a haunted glimmer in Roman's eyes, and it pushed Wyatt to ask a question he otherwise may not have.

"What happened?"

Roman shook his head, flipping that tight-lipped grimace back into an easy grin. The fucker knew how to turn it on, Wyatt would give him that. He could see exactly why this charismatic and easygoing man (until the guns started going off, that is) could lead a group across an international hunt for the pages to... a book? Wyatt still wasn't sure how this tome would lead them all to infinite riches, but that didn't seem to matter. Roman's gravitational pull worked to tie them all together regardless.

"That's a story for another day," Roman answered, nodding toward the exit. Wyatt made a mental bookmark to be sure to circle back. He realized that there were years and years of stories left untold between them. Where had Roman been? What had this wild life done to him? Who had he met? Worked with? Loved?

So many questions, and knowing Roman, Wyatt wasn't getting any of those answers soon.

"Let's head back. I feel like that moray eel's been watching us this entire time."

Wyatt looked to a small cove created in the coral, where a huge moray hung with its head out and a weird smile on its prehistoric-looking green face. "Yeah, he's giving me creepy pervert vibes. Are we sure there aren't cameras here? I think he might have set some up."

Roman laughed, an arm around Wyatt's lower back as they walked out of the underwater tunnel. "I'm glad I've got my saltshaker here. This all feels right. Like it was meant to happen this way."

Wyatt secretly *glowed* at hearing his old nickname again, the warmth spreading through him like the roots of an ancient tree, burrowing deep. He didn't show how happy hearing that made him, not yet, but he did allow the smile to grow, pushing at his cheeks and forming two dimples that were rarely ever on display.

He went to sleep with that same grin—and woke up with it, too.

Chapter 11

Roman Ashford

THE PLANE TOUCHED down in Madrid sometime after four o'clock local time, a private jet that had been hired to take a "film crew" to the location of their next shoot. They deplaned and hopped right into the waiting van. Roman enjoyed spoiling his gang, especially now that they had an official name to tie them together.

Too bad this was meant to be their last job. He thought the Rainbow's Seven had a nice ring to it.

He also appreciated how well everyone gelled together. Even Wyatt, being the newest and most reluctant member, found a friend in Bang Bang, who played blackjack with him to help keep Wyatt's mind off his fear of flying. Roman also offered his assistance by shooting him a text to meet him in the bathroom, where he could help distract him some more, but Wyatt sent an eye-roll emoji and said "too obvious."

Roman didn't really care if it was obvious or not. Their hookup at the aquarium unlocked a feral side to him, keeping his dick in a constantly chubbed state, not helped by the fact that erections seemed to spontaneously appear for men flying thirty-six thousand feet up in the air.

But Roman also respected Wyatt enough to not push. He shot back a crying face and left it at that, getting lost in a conversation with Doc and Phantom over the benefits of going gluten-free, not exactly the most riveting conversation but one that Roman ran with nonetheless. The mundane topic helped keep his thoughts from circling back to Wyatt coming down his throat.

"We're here," Mimic said from the passenger seat as Mustang pulled up to the five-star hotel they were staying at, only minutes from where the party was being held. Wyatt let out a low (but still audible) "holy fucking shit" as he stepped out of the car, Roman holding the door open for him.

"Not bad, huh? Wait until you see the rooms." Roman put a hand between Wyatt's shoulders and walked with him toward the golden doors, a series of different flags waving above them. There was a golden tiger just behind the valet station, which was crowded with men and women wearing designer suits and dresses, all of them likely headed to the same party. The towering columns on either side of the entrance appeared to have been brought in from the coliseum itself, spiraling up toward the clear blue sky.

Roman and Wyatt walked through the sliding glass doors, Mimic coming up on Roman's side. Her usual raven black hair was now luscious auburn brown waves that fell down to her back, a pair of expensive Gucci sunglasses sitting on a perfectly sculpted nose, her high cheekbones sparkling from a dash of crystal-like highlight. She looped an arm through Roman's and smiled at the front desk, checking them in using fluent Spanish. Roman knew just enough to get by, but his accent would likely give away his non-native speaking tongue, which wouldn't be ideal considering they were supposed to be close relatives to the birthday girl.

The smiling concierge gave them all a bubbling glass of champagne with their room keys and walked them to their own private elevator. They were staying in the two presidential suites, connected at the very top floor of the hotel, making it a surprisingly long ride in the red velvet elevator.

The doors dinged open and dropped them off in a small lobby, decked out in an eclectic collection of furniture. There was an antique table painted purple in front of a sitting area that was framed by a palm-tree-covered wallpaper, and a small love seat that appeared to be a red high-heel shoe, sitting under-

The Sunset Job

neath an opulent chandelier. It bordered on the tacky but leaned closer to the artsy, and Roman fucking loved it. He was reminded of the wild shit his neighbors at the trailer park would bring home, decorating their front lawns with upcycled Christmas decorations and items from abandoned storage containers. He imagined this would be what their places would look if they had the money backing this bougie-ass hotel.

The suites did not buck the trend, being just as extravagantly wild in the furniture and decoration choices, creating plenty of opportunities for the perfect photo op. Mimic thanked the bellman, the couple of suitcases they'd brought set outside of the girls' room. Doc lifted her Beats, loud rock music bleeding from the pink headphones, and set them around her neck, racing past Mustang and Mimic to get first dibs on the room.

"Damn, Monica, you're going to let Doc beat you like that?" Phantom asked, ribbing her as he grabbed his book bag from the golden cart. Roman laughed, walking to their suite and holding the door open for Bang Bang and Wyatt.

"These feet are only made to race on wheels. She can have whatever room she wants. I'm probably just going to end up crashing in Mimic's anyway."

"Oh really?" Mimic asked, arching a brow, painted red lips curling into a smile.

"Yeah, remember you promised to tutor me in French? That's going to take all night."

Mimic narrowed her smokey eyes, chuckling as she turned and walked into the suite, her skintight black jeans looking like liquid paint against her long legs.

Mustang dropped her sunglasses and shook her head. "Merci," she said, following Mimic into the suite. Phantom turned to Roman, shaking his head.

"Mustang's going to come out of that room speaking all kinds of nasty shit in French."

"At least she'll sound classy doing it," Roman quipped.

"Truth." Phantom gave an appreciative butt slap as he walked past Roman and into the room. "Thanks for all this, by the way. You're a solid boss."

"You guys deserve it for putting up with all my crazy shit."

"Hey, your crazy shit's paid off so far. Let's keep it going, man."

"I plan on it, Axle. Now go grab a room and get ready. We've got a quinceañera to crash. Nice watch by the way." Roman motioned toward the golden wristwatch shining on Phantom's wrist.

"Thanks, man. My sister got it for me as a gift for a, well, I'll tell you later."

Roman nodded, smiling as Phantom left to get ready, the start of this sunset job already on the horizon.

The Sunset Job

* * *

The group reunited in the girls' suite, gathering in the opulent living room, most of them decked out in designer outfits, looking nearly unrecognizable from their casual international flight attire from hours earlier. Roman couldn't help but embrace the vanity and think to himself:

Damn, we're one hot fucking crew.

He admired all of them but had to work extra hard to hide his attraction toward Wyatt. The guy cleaned up well. *Real* well. Not that he was working with anything negative to begin with, but seeing him in a pair of acid-washed jeans and a clean white V-neck shirt, his hair gelled and his face still moist from the shower, it lit that fire in Roman's belly again, the flames catching and spreading downward.

"Alright, my queens and my kings, it's almost showtime. I don't think I have to go over every step of the plan with you all; just know that we need the page Giovanni is carrying on him, and we need to grab it at all costs. He's keeping that page as a favor to his dead lover, but if he realizes how badly we want it, he might just put it through a paper shredder and be done with it. We need that page."

"Phantom and I go in first, right?" Bang Bang sat on the couch with an arm thrown over Doc's shoulder, her head resting on the crook of his neck. He was dressed in all white, a chef's hat on his lap and a catering company name badge pinned to his chest. They seemed to be getting closer by the hour. Again, not exactly ideal since personal relations could bleed into the job and fuck things up, but Roman definitely wasn't one to say anything about inter-crew relations. He was almost jealous of the two, wondering how Wyatt would feel if it was them two cozied up on the couch together.

"Correct. You two go in and work the kitchen, figure out the dining arrangements and if there's a chance of us getting Giovanni alone, before or after. We just need to get him alone so we can kindly ask him for the page with the trigger phrase, and if he doesn't kindly reply, then we get a little rougher. If any of you see a chance to lift it off of him without him realizing, all the better." Roman cracked his knuckles, the silver rings on his hand catching the light from the movie-set-style lamp behind the teal couch.

"Wyatt, Doc, you two are staying put. Wyatt, you worked on getting into their camera system on the flight here. Were you successful?"

Wyatt nodded, lips pursed. "Took me five minutes. People need to invest in firewalls, or at least passwords that don't include birthdays." He wasn't proud, Roman could tell from the slump in his shoulders, but he had done it.

"Oh crap. Not this." Mimic shot up from the couch, pulling everyone's attention as she read the message she'd just received. Mustang rose with her, eyebrows knitting together, reassuring hand moving to her elbow.

"What? What is it?" Roman could tell this was bad, whatever *this* was, he just wasn't sure how bad.

"I just got a message from one of my connects. Security's been made aware of a possible man and woman thief pair coming in as fake husband and wife. Fuck."

Roman reared back as if he'd been struck. "How? This shit should have been airtight."

Mimic offered no answers in her shocked expression. Roman looked around the gathered group, weighing them all in a slightly different light. Was there a leak in the Rainbow's Seven? Were they all playing for the same team, or was something rotten in the group?

He took a deep breath, unable to crack that question right now. He had to focus on the job instead: getting into the party and taking that page.

"Fine," Roman said, eyes settling on a confused-looking Wyatt. "Then let them expect a husband and wife. We'll just go in as husband and husband instead."

Chapter 12

Wyatt Hernandez

Wyatt couldn't help but walk down the cobblestone path with his back a little straighter than usual, his chin a little higher, the expensive suit forming to his body like something a Power Ranger would wear to go fight a city-razing monster. He was used to wearing the museum uniform (a pair of khakis and three gray polos that were desperately needing to be replaced) and switching into a pair of gym shorts and some old graphic tees, his uniform for lounging at home.

Yet here he was, about to be brushing elbows with the Spanish elite, wearing an outfit that cost more than the down payment on a tiny condo.

It not only helped him feel more confident but also helped ease some of the nerves that came with this last-minute change in plans. He had been mentally preparing to hang out with Doc in the room, watching surveillance cameras and eating way too many sour jelly beans for anyone's own good, washing them down with way too much champagne.

Instead, Wyatt was standing at the ivy-draped entrance to Alcázar of Segovia, a castle about an hour's drive from Madrid, perched on top of a rocky crag and flanked by two rivers, the Guadarrama mountains rising behind it as if made to watch over the ancient fortress. They had to cross over a moat and make it past a security checkpoint in the front courtyard, their fake invites created by Mimic passing the test and granting them access. The guards didn't look twice at the handsome gay couple there to attend their distant niece's extravagant birthday party.

"Keep your eyes peeled," Roman said, leaning in close to Wyatt and whispering in his ear, his breath creating a ripple of tingles that dripped down his spine. "Giovanni should be wearing a navy blue suit with a pink rose pinned to the lapel."

"Got it," Wyatt replied, smiling at the attendant.

"Bienvenidos, chicos," the woman said, holding out a program with the schedule for the evening. Roman looked to Wyatt, who was fluent in Spanish even though his Cuban accent would give him away as a non-native. It was better than Roman fumbling for words and getting lost in translation, so they decided Wyatt would take point in most conversations.

"Alright," Wyatt said, walking up to Roman, who waited for him next to a marble statue of a dancing woman, her stone silk skirts flowing as if in actual motion. "She said the main party is happening in the Hall of the Galley, with these four rooms set up as smaller party rooms playing different kinds of music. In three hours, everyone's supposed to gather for a dance in the Hall of Kings, featuring the birthday girl and a court of her closest friends and family, so we might have the best chance of bumping into Giovanni then."

"He'll be surrounded by people," Roman said, smiling and nodding at a couple walking by with their two starry-eyed daughters in tow. "We need another window. Are there any restricted areas to the castle?"

"Oh, tons. Everything on this map marked with an X. She told me they'd be roped off, too."

"Perfect, we'll have to lure him into one of those areas." Roman tapped his earpiece, activating the mic. "Bang Bang, Phantom, how's the kitchen looking?"

Bang Bang's voice buzzed into Wyatt's skull. "A fucking mess. No one here even knows how to cook a proper scallop. Shit's like rubber, *broki*."

"Forget about the food. What about Giovanni? He's a VIP—he should have someone catering to his meals. Find them, and then follow them."

The Sunset Job

"We're looking," Bang Bang said through his loud chewing.

Wyatt pointed down the long hallway, ornate tapestries made with rich wool and silk lining the length of the sun-washed hall. "Should we start looking, too?" Music could be heard drifting from a set of open double doors, partygoers milling about a snacks table before entering. There was a mix of people, mostly rich and spoiled children, having the time of their lives, doing their best *Downton Abbey* impressions. Their parents formed loose social bubbles that floated from group to group, mother and fathers chatting about upcoming vacations, political trends, weather updates.

None of them appeared to be their target.

"Let's go," Roman said, reaching out his hand and smoothly twining his fingers between Wyatt's. It sent a flare of heat directly through his chest, like an arrow dipped in flames shot from atop one of the many spiraling gold columns surrounding them. He tried not to overthink it. This was part of the job—they were meant to act as if they were married; any auxiliary feelings that came along with their act only enhanced the lie. Perfect. Then, once they had the page in their possession and this leg of the job was over, Wyatt would go back to keeping his hands tucked firmly in his pockets, away from Roman's perfectly firm and slightly calloused and deliciously warm grip.

But for now, he just had to suck it up and hold Roman's hand in his. However would he survive?

...

Just fine, apparently. They walked all throughout the packed Hall of the Galley, named because of how the castle was built to resemble the bow of a sailing ship, hand in hand and eyes peeled for their target, not spotting him anywhere in the throng of dancing kids and slightly drunk adults. Wyatt spoke to a handful of people in hopes of getting any wind of where Giovanni might be, but none seemed to have any clear answer. They did one more spin around the main room before looking into the three adjacent ones without any success.

They stepped through an arching side door and into a poppy-filled garden, the mountains looming in the distance, the cracked stone walls surrounding them pocked with bright green moss. "Where the hell is this guy?" Wyatt asked, Roman taking his hand back and leaving Wyatt's with the outline of his warmth. He didn't like how much he immediately missed it.

Roman tapped the earpiece. "Boys, updates?"

Moments later, Phantom replied. "Nothing, boss. The only person here with a private chef is the birthday girl. No one knows where Giovanni is."

"Alright, I need you two to grab a platter of hors d'oeuvres and walk around. Get lost and look around the restricted areas. Maybe he's slipped away for some reason."

"Got it." The mic gave a little buzz of static as the connection cut.

"He is here, right?" Wyatt asked, arms crossed and eyes tilted up, squinting against the sun and locking onto Roman's crystal-green gaze.

"All our intel says he is, unless he got scared off by the high-alert status the guards seem to be on."

"What if we can't find him?"

"We will. One way or another. We need that page."

Wyatt decided to poke a little harder. "Why? What's so special about a couple of pages?"

Roman's sea-glass-green eyes tilted upward, away from Wyatt. He chewed on the inside of his cheek. What the hell was he being so cagey about? It frustrated Wyatt, who was the one who should have his guard up around the charismatic but double-edged personality that was Roman Ashford. Wyatt was the one who deserved an apology on hands and knees from the man who'd fucked up his entire life, and yet that same man couldn't even be fully transparent with him about what they were after?

Such bullshit.

The anger bubbled up to Wyatt's lips, forming a string of words without any proper thought behind them. "Why are you such a secretive asshole? Out of everyone working this job, I should be the one you trust the most. Yes, we've had some fucked-up crap happen to us, and that's made me wary but not untrustworthy."

Roman licked his lips, eyes narrowing, his thoughts swirling as clear as the flecks of bright emerald in his eyes. "I just have to be cautious about certain things, that's all. Nothing to do with how much I trust you."

"Really? Because you're acting like you trust me just as much as a dog trusts a vet holding a rectal thermometer."

Roman cocked his head and smirked. "I think you'd like that a little more than the dog would."

"Oh, shut up," Wyatt said, shaking his head and rolling his eyes. He was about to rebut with a joke about Roman needing more than a thermometer but swallowed his joke with a surprised jolt, his eyes nearly bulging out of his skull when he realized who he'd just spotted.

"Roman," he said, hushed. "Look. It's him."

Roman followed Wyatt's gaze. Sure enough, standing there all by himself in his navy suit with his pink rose, swirling a flute of champagne underneath an ivy-covered gazebo, was Giovanni Gorga. The man of the hour, the target for tonight. Wyatt's pulse spiked, his heart kicking off a race against no one but himself.

"Let's go introduce ourselves," Roman said, reaching for Wyatt's hand again, encasing it in his. It did nothing to help with the anxiety. The pressure mounted with every step they took, bringing them closer to an oblivious Giovanni. Yes, Roman had made it clear he could take the page with force (and would if his back was against the wall), but that wasn't the way this was meant to go. Roman wanted to talk his way through this without needing to draw a gun or throw a punch, and that meant Wyatt would have to think on his toes and improv his way through whatever conversation came next.

Just "yes, and" everything. It'll all be fine. Totally fine.

Unfortunately for the three men—but primarily so for Giovanni—all would actually be very, very, *very* far from fine.

Chapter 13

Roman Ashford

"Giovanni, hola." Wyatt approached first, sporting a friendly smile and holding out his hand for a shake. Giovanni looked up from his phone and cocked his head, sizing up the two men. His eyes darted over Roman's shoulders, likely wondering where his security guards were.

Roman wondered the same thing but couldn't dwell on it. This was it, their target. Somewhere on Giovanni's person was the page they came here looking for. The easy part of this job was over; now came the hard part.

"You are?" Giovanni asked in a heavily accented English.

"I'm Teddy, and this is my husband, Sam," Wyatt said, using their cover names. As if to sell their story a little better, Wyatt cuddled into Roman's side, resting his head on Roman's shoulder for a brief moment. He was really selling this act, huh?

And were the butterflies cropping up in Roman's chest part of the act, too?

Nah. Probably not.

"We're Beatriz's guncles."

Going off Giovanni's confused (and increasingly annoyed) expression, Wyatt explained further. "Gay uncles. We're the ones who get to spoil her rotten and not deal with any of the consequences of that."

"I know what 'guncles' are," Giovanni said, still looking annoyed but also less confused. "I just came out here to get fresh air. I should be getting back inside."

"Actually," Roman said, stepping in front of Giovanni and blocking his path. He had to switch up strategies. "I've been hoping we'd bump into each other."

"You have?" Giovanni's bushy brows inched together.

"Yes, there's a lot of talk in this family, I'm sure you know that. And there were rumors that hit a little close to home. About you and Remy and how he was mistreating you."

Giovanni's green eyes expanded. "Mistreating me? Absolutely not, no. Remy was my other half. He was my everything... how do you know him?"

Roman nodded, lips pursed. He wanted to strike an emotional nerve in the man, knock him off his balance. He also knew there wasn't much time before his security guards came looking for him, which would further complicate the situation. If he had to throw a punch to grab the papers, he would have preferred to do that without any gun-toting guards present.

"He was my lover," Roman said, sending a visible jolt up Giovanni's spine.

"He—we did explore, but he never spoke about someone who looked like you... Lover? When?" Giovanni's eyes darted to Wyatt, whose face gave nothing away. Roman made a mental note to compliment the freckle-faced poker player.

"A year before he passed. We met during one of his TED Talks." It actually wasn't a lie at all. Roman and Remy had hooked up—not exactly the best lay of Roman's life, but definitely the most life-changing one—and that same night was when Roman was told about the two pages that would rock his entire world. Remy was drunk off three bottles of Dom and high off two lines of coke, all leading the modern-day Nostradamus down a rambling road that revealed the treasure hunt he had decided to leave behind, already knowing he didn't have much time left on this earth.

Remy had also given Roman a key phrase that night, one that he promised would make sense when spoken to whoever held the pages. "He told me: gold always glitters under a full moon."

The Sunset Job

Giovanni's jaw dropped. Recognition filtered in through his shocked gaze, his hand absentmindedly floating over the chest of his navy suit, the pink rose pinned to the lapel looking fake with how perfect it was. That must be where he kept it. It took a heavy amount of willpower for Roman to keep his hands at his side. "He always said..."

"The page from the tome. We need it." Roman took a step forward, glancing to his side. Wyatt was tense, his shoulders showing the slightest tremble in them, only recognizable because Roman knew what to look for.

"I've been holding on to this since he died. I promised him to keep it safe, only giving it to the person who would be meant to have it. He took such good care of me, this was the least I could do. He told me the phrase would show me who that person was." Giovanni slipped a hand under his suit. Roman wanted to spring in the air and tap his heels together at how smoothly this had all gone. There were about a thousand different ways this leg of the job could have gone tits up, but somehow, Roman managed to avoid all of them, the finish line clear as day.

Wyatt smiled, too, likely experiencing the same relief as Roman was.

And then it all went to complete shit in a burning handbasket.

Two loud gunshots echoed from behind them, the spray of falling glass clattering against the floor filling the stunned silence, followed by the release of a room full of screams, shrill and panicked. Roman knew exactly who was behind the shots and looked to Giovanni and Wyatt as he unholstered his gun from under his suit. "Take cover," he told both of them before looking to Wyatt, his big brown eyes blown wide with panic. "Keep him safe."

"I will," he said.

"Do you know how to shoot a gun?"

Wyatt nodded. "I went to the range a couple of times with an old fling. Absolutely hated it."

"Good. Here." Roman handed him his pistol, reaching for the second one he had on him. "I don't know where Giovanni's security is, but I'm going to take a guess and say those bullets were for them." Before Roman left the garden, he grabbed Wyatt and kissed him, briefly but with a force that required no spoken words once their lips parted.

Wyatt ran with Giovanni to the edge of the garden, crouching behind a stone statue of a hunter holding out a taut bow. It would provide ample enough coverage, which was great considering the fact that three masked men burst into the gardens at that exact moment. Shots rang through the air as Roman dove behind a fountain, its spitting head blown clean off and sending shards of stone flying in all directions.

Roman braced himself against the ridge of the

fountain, peeking over and taking a shot. One of the men dropped with an anguished cry.

Great, two left.

Another series of gunshots went off, bullets hitting the fountain. Roman's ears rang, and his vision pulsed. Adrenaline worked to sharpen his senses, picking up on a brief silence as the men reloaded, leaving themselves open.

Rookie fucking mistake.

Roman took the bait—and bait it was. Neither of them was reloading, one of them having gone around the gardens and was now crouched feet away from Wyatt and Giovanni's hiding place while the other took aim.

Roman dove back down, dodging the bullet by a hair's width. "Wyatt, from your left," he shouted in warning, hoping to all hope that Wyatt could use that gun. A few loud bangs erupted from that corner of the garden, and Roman braced himself as he called out, "Are you okay?"

Seconds—or a couple of eternities, hard to tell—ticked by before Wyatt answered. "Yeah, we're okay, we're good. He's down."

Roman breathed a sigh of relief, able to return his focus to the lone shooter. He was masked, wearing all black, making it easier to spot the long necklace that hung off the man's neck, a lion's tooth held in a steel cage inches from his heart. Roman knew to aim there, use it same as he would a bullseye at the range.

He steadied his breath, braced his muscles. The cold metal of the gun felt like an extension of himself, as if he could guide the bullet to the target with his fingers alone. Another steady breath, lungs full, pulse slowing.

Roman stood from his cover and pressed down on the trigger. Two shots exploded at the same time. The masked assailant's bullet missed, hitting the wall behind Roman.

Roman's aim wasn't anywhere nearly as bad. The man dropped like a bag of lead, crumpling to the ground as blood pooled around his head.

That's it. They'd done it. Neutralized the threats and salvaged their hit. He ran to Wyatt and Giovanni, both of them crouched on the ground, with Wyatt using his body to shield the panicked man. The gun was still in Wyatt's hands, his knuckles pale from how hard he was holding on to it.

"You're good, you're safe," Roman said, taking the gun from Wyatt and helping him back to his feet, holding both hands in his. He squeezed, kissing Wyatt's forehead. The trembles in his shoulders hadn't gone anywhere, but they did seem to lessen now that the gunshots had stopped flying. "You did good, saltshaker."

"That's such a shitty nickname compared to everyone else," Wyatt said, his head falling into Roman's chest, his lungs tugging in a deep breath. "Can it just be Salt? That sounds pretty cool." His

The Sunset Job

words were slightly muffled against Roman's shirt, but he still understood every single one of them.

"Salt it is." Roman kissed the top of Wyatt's head before turning his attention to Giovanni. "You aren't hurt, are you?"

"No, no. I'm okay. Thank you for that—you both saved me." A man ran into the garden, suited like the guests but holding a jet-black pistol like he was a trained soldier. Roman raised his gun and locked the man in his sights, finger grazing the trigger.

A hand closed around his wrist. "No," Giovanni said. "That's Berto, my security." Giovanni then reached into an inner pocket hidden in his suit and pulled out a neatly folded piece of thick paper, the edges aged with a tint of brown. Roman lowered his gun and reached for the prize. The sun was already beginning to set, but to Roman, the paper glowed as if spotlit by a direct beam of afternoon sunlight.

His fingers closed around the paper. Giovanni smiled, appearing relieved, happy—and when a muted pop sounded—shocked, stunned, blood trickling from his lip. He fell to his knees, letting go of the paper and clutching the blood-soaked fabric of his chest.

His "security guard" stood with the gun now aimed at Roman. "I'm going to need that piece of paper."

Chapter 14

Wyatt Hernandez

Roman shifted slightly so that the gun was aimed at him and not a trembling Wyatt. This wasn't anywhere in the plans, a heart-stopping fear washing over him with the realization. Not only had he just shot and likely killed someone, but now he was facing the opposite end of the gun and had no idea what to do about it.

"Just give him the page," Wyatt said through the pounds of sand that had been teleported into his mouth and throat.

"Listen to your boyfriend." The man moved closer, pressing the pistol into Roman's chest. Wyatt looked down, seeing the gun he used back in the holster on Roman's hip. If he inched his hand a little to the left, he could graze his fingertips against the cold steel. But he'd have to be incredibly quick if he wanted to get off a shot without the man blowing Roman's chest wide open.

Impossible. He couldn't do it. His shoulders shook, and he tried to force them to still, making them tremble further.

"You're working for the Pride?" Roman asked, paper still in his hand.

"I'm working for whoever pays the highest." A manic glare entered the man's beady black eyes. Wyatt knew this was the end. They had messed up, and it would cost them their lives.

"Did someone pay you to stand in front of the huntress statue in the gardens? With a gun aimed at my heart?"

"Someone paid me to shut you the fuck up." The man drove a knee up and into Roman's crotch, making him gasp and clutch at his stomach, the page still in his tight grip.

"Alright, fine. I didn't want any more blood, but you forced my hand."

A single gunshot blasted through the air. Wyatt shouted, looking to Roman and trying to discern where the bullet had entered. Maybe it was a clean wound, entrance and exit, through some nonvital part of him. Maybe... Roman wasn't bleeding. He hadn't been shot.

The man who'd had them cornered grabbed at his chest before his knees gave way. He collapsed at their feet, lifeless by the time he hit the ground.

Bang Bang's voice echoed in Wyatt's skull. "Thanks for the location assist, *broki*. Meet us out front? Mustang's waiting."

"We'll see you there," Roman responded, waving up at the window Bang Bang had just been at before stepping over the body and encasing Wyatt in a tight embrace. "Come on, Salt. Let's get the fuck out of here."

A small part of Wyatt—the part that wasn't dealing with a brain-numbing amount of shock—felt an electric buzz course through him at the use of his nickname. He smiled against Roman's chest, allowing himself a second to soak in the man's warmth before pulling away. Roman put the folded-up page into the pocket of his suit and grabbed Wyatt's hand before they took off, running past the bonsai trees and the azaleas and the poppies, a blur of colors swishing behind them as they burst into the castle, falling directly into a chaotic scene. Terrified parents were shielding crying children, running for whatever exit was the closest, security guards having completely lost control of the scene.

Better for them, Roman and Wyatt easily blending into the tangle of party guests trying to escape. They flowed through the tapestry-lined hall and through the massive doors, out into the night air. Mustang smiled at them from behind the wheel of a ruby-red Mercedes, Bang Bang already in the passenger seat and drinking a dew-covered Corona.

Roman hurried to the door and opened it. Wyatt threw himself into the back of the car and fell against Phantom. Roman got in and completed the sandwich, the door slamming shut as Mustang slammed on the gas, the momentum pushing Wyatt back into the white leather seats.

"Did you get it?" Mustang asked, eyes piercing through the rearview mirror.

"I got it," Roman said, taking the page out and lifting it in the air.

"Fuck. Yes. Party in the girls' room tonight," Mustang said as the boys gave celebratory hoots, Phantom reaching over and patting Roman's leg. Wyatt was no longer shaking. Instead, he found himself smiling as they drove through the Spanish countryside, the entire ride full of them trying to out-sing the other and failing miserably.

* * *

The mood in the girls' suite was purely celebratory, with loud music blaring through the speakers and four buckets of unopened champagne sitting in their ice baths, waiting for the group to finish drinking the one they were currently passing around, taking swigs directly from the bottle. Wyatt was last, the bubbly gold champagne going down like silk. He lifted the empty bottle to a room of cheers, Roman slapping him square in the back.

"We did it, gang," Roman said over the clapping and cheering. "We just need to do this one more time, and then we grab the book and we have our entire lives changed forever."

"To the Rainbow's Seven," Mimic said, raising a glass of rosé up into the sky. Wyatt grabbed his beer and joined the circle in the center of the room, clinking their glasses together. As much as Wyatt still doubted his decision to say yes to one of Roman's crazy schemes, it was moments like these that made it seem worth it. He was risking a lot by being here, but the reward was already beginning to show.

The rest of the night played out like a scene in one of Wyatt's favorite movies. They danced and played games, talked and laughed and joked. They played drinking games and teased each other like a group of old friends would, the invisible bonds between the seven growing stronger and stronger as the night wore on.

Sometime around midnight, Wyatt found himself having a deep heart-to-heart with Phantom on the balcony, overlooking the glittering city of Madrid. The air was refreshing, and the honesty between them even more so.

"Yeah," Phantom said, leaning on the iron balcony, a row of potted plants hanging off the other end. "Me and my sister are really tight. She's my best friend."

"Same with me and mine," Wyatt replied. He'd

already drunk enough to make his limbs a little stringy and his lips a little looser. "Life kind of made sure we stuck together. Our parents died when we were both barely teens, and the rest of our family was either struggling with their own demons or too selfish to help with ours. Shit sucked, but me and Julie made it through okay."

"Damn, man, your story sounds pretty similar to mine. My dad passed, but my mom married a man who completely changed her. It's almost like we lost her with our dad." Phantom turned, crossing an arm across his chest and drinking from his glass of white wine. He wore an orange tank top with a trio of Greek letters printed across the front, the fraternity's pool party advertised underneath by a seemingly drunk seal, a bra hanging off its neck. "It definitely pushed me and my sister together. We became inseparable, which was exactly why my stepdad tried to separate us. We learned how to work together after that. She's actually helping out on this job, just remotely."

"Really? What's she doing?"

"She'll be important in getting the tome. She's a curator at a museum in Los Angeles. She's making sure the *Writing Through the Ages* exhibit lands on her doorstep so that we'll have a way easier time of grabbing it. She'll of course get a cut, and she needs it. Her daughter—she's going through it medically. She's got a rare bone cancer, and the treatment price is wild. And there's an experimental drug that she wants to try on top of the treatments, she just doesn't have the money to."

Wyatt's smile faded, his heart growing heavy while also feeling slightly more connected to Phantom.

"I'm glad you two are close, then. This job is for her, too."

"Yeah, she's a good one... Guess that's why I came out to her a few days ago."

It took a second for the words to register in Wyatt's alcohol-dulled brain. His eyebrows shot up before he brought his expression back to neutral.

"She's the first person I've told. Got me this watch as a coming-out gift. Use to be our dad's, but she got it fixed up after she found it in the attic. And now you're the second person I've told." Phantom smiled, eyes crinkling as he lifted his glass. "Cheers."

"Thank you for telling me," Wyatt said, returning the smile as he drank the last of his beer. "I personally know how hard the first few times are."

"First few *times*?"

Wyatt nodded, lips pursing. "Oh yeah, coming out never stops. You'll be 'coming out' until the day you're 'heading out.' It's just the curse we have to carry for being so fucking fabulous. And so great at taking dick."

Phantom almost spat out his mouthful of wine.

The Sunset Job

"Sorry," Wyatt said, blushing. "It's the drinks talking."

Phantom gave him a look before cracking up, doubling over with the wave of laughter, the fit catching on to Wyatt.

"Seriously, though," Wyatt said, working hard to control the bubbling laughs. "It means a lot to be one of those first few people. And it does get easier, that I can also promise you."

"It actually hasn't been that hard. When I told my sister, it was over a bunch of left-over Chinese food with *Survivor* playing in the background, and all she said was 'Axle, I love you no matter who you love. Now, can we please watch to see who wins the immunity challenge?'"

"And that's how it should be, honestly. As simple and basic as 'this is who I am, thanks for listening, goodbye.' Sucks that it isn't that way for so many people. Kids especially."

Phantom shook his head, tilting his gaze up toward the starless sky. "Yeah, I'm not sure how my mom's going to take it. Definitely not as easy as my sister, not with the way I was raised. Toxic masculinity isn't exactly a stranger in the Black community, and my mom unfortunately soaked in all the bullshit the men around her put out. Then there's the fact that she loves a good church Sunday. Plus, I know she'll start worrying about what my aunts and uncles and cousins and everyone else under the fucking sun would say... yeah, that's going to be difficult."

Wyatt looked at this man, someone who had seen his fair share of life-threatening situations and likely stared them all down with the brave face of a roaring lion. Yet there was fear in his big brown eyes when he spoke about coming out to his own mother, someone who should love him unconditionally, no matter what religion she believed in or who her son brought into bed with him. Unconditional and unending love, and yet Phantom was scared, scared to reveal one of the most genuine parts of himself to her.

It weighed heavy on Wyatt's heart. He felt lucky enough to have come out to his mother before she passed and to have her love and support rained down on him. She didn't bat an eyelash, only hugged and kissed him. He wished Phantom could have that same experience but wasn't quite sure if it was in his future.

"At least you've got the crew behind you," Wyatt said, trying to find a light in the darkness. "You know coming out to them is going to be easy."

"Pfft, I'm sure being 'straight' around them was harder than being gay will ever be."

Wyatt and Phantom both devolved back into a fit of laughter, the two cementing a solid foundation for their friendship.

"Roman's one of the reasons why I felt comfort-

The Sunset Job

able enough coming out," Phantom revealed. "The comfort that man has in his own skin, it's enviable. I wanted that. I remember meeting him, years ago, at a casino in Vegas. He made the room stop when he walked in, like he was James Bond himself. I was actually being arrested that night—" Wyatt guffawed at the whiplash in the story. "Long story, but he saw me when I slipped out of the handcuffs as if they were made of butter. He followed me and asked me to work with him on a job for a nice percentage. Never stopped working with him since. And he's never lost that cocky confidence, either."

"No, no he hasn't."

The pair stayed out on the balcony for a little longer, joking about Phantom earning his queer quota before the end of the month, both of them laughing until tears rolled and bellies ached.

Chapter 15

Roman Ashford

Roman sat in the love seat closest to the fireplace, just underneath a portrait of a dappled horse standing in the center of a field of lavender. He quite liked that painting, feeling a sense of comfort whenever he looked at it with the swirling purples and light greens. He wasn't the kind of guy that could spend hours strolling through an art museum, but he definitely appreciated the technique and effort that went into creating the painting, framed with a thin gold border.

Much less work had gone into creating the page he had in his hands, and yet it was also immensely more valuable than the painting ever would be.

He couldn't believe it. One piece of the puzzle was now in his hands. He read it over for the hundredth time, tossing over each word as if it were a pebble hiding a diamond underneath.

The Sunset Job

It was a page from early on in the book. It was an introduction, explaining the methods behind Remy's madness. He wrote with a witty self-awareness that welcomed the reader in, lowered their guard, and allowed them to believe that anything Remy might say would come to pass, one way or another. It fascinated Roman, especially considering that many of the things he wrote about *did* become actuality. Yes, much of it was vague assumptions of the future that could be interpreted in a handful of different ways, but some of his predictions hit the bullseye in a way that could only be described as premonitions.

He focused on the last line, committing that one to memory. A fire could break out and the page could turn to ash, and it wouldn't matter, so long as Roman remembered that one line.

The fourth January second in the twentieth century will bring riches beyond anyone's imagination.

To most, it was likely gibberish, but to Roman, it was everything.

Two low knocks pulled his attention up toward the arching stone door with its golden handle. Roman's bedroom was the largest of the crew's, with an attached library that had a nook covered in some of the most comfortable cushions Roman had ever felt. He got up, setting the page inside of the cabinet next to the bed.

"Come in."

The door opened, and he expected to see Mimic or Bang Bang, both of whom usually had trouble sleeping and liked to talk shit with him until their eyes got heavy.

Instead, it was Wyatt, standing there with the warm light of the lamps washing over him. He wore a pair of light gray sleeping shorts and a black T-shirt, his glasses on and his hair tousled in a couple of different directions.

"Busy?" Wyatt asked, peeking in.

"No, no. Just having some wine before bed. Want a glass?"

"Sure," he said, stepping into the room. "Damn, this is massive."

"I kind of wish this wasn't our last night here." Roman pulled a dewy bottle of wine from the ice bucket and poured a glass, bringing it over to Wyatt as he admired a marble statue of an elephant, spider-web-thin cracks spreading across its tusks and ears.

"Good job today." Roman looked into Wyatt's eyes, committing each fleck of golden brown to memory. "For someone who rarely shoots a gun, you handled yourself exceptionally well."

"Thanks," he said, taking a big drink of his wine. "I still can't even process it. It's like my servers are bugging out or something."

"Taking someone's life is never easy, even if it's in self-defense. It'll take some time to really sink it. But when it does, and when you're ready, I'm here to talk about it. Getting it out of your system helps. It really does."

Wyatt smiled, his lips disappearing as he took another drink. "Thanks, Roman." He went over to the dark blue couch set on golden tiger claws. He took a seat, sinking back into the plush cushion. "So, do you want to tell me why you've been so secretive? How did you even get that phrase? Was what you said true?"

Roman moved to sit down next to Wyatt, finding it difficult to resist the magnetic pull that existed between them. Like two celestial bodies rotating around the same sun, their paths destined to crash. Would that be tonight?

"It was. I got it from Remy himself. I, well, hooked up with him, like I said, and he ended up spilling it all to me. There's other ways of finding the phrases, not just through dicking down the creator of this crazy egg hunt."

Wyatt scoffed, shaking his head. He drank, his Adam's apple bobbing with his sips. The room became a couple of degrees hotter for Roman. He sat up, adjusting himself.

"What's the next phrase?" Wyatt asked, his gaze focused on a vase overflowing with peonies.

Roman knew this was a test. Wyatt was dipping his toes in the opaque pool of information Roman tried to keep to himself. He valued the idea of holding as many cards close to his chest as possible, especially considering the possibility of a leak in their otherwise tight-knit crew. It worried Roman and made him want to keep quiet about everything except the most vital pieces of information.

"Listen to the blue jays sing. It's like paradise."

Wyatt blinked, cocked his head.

"That's it, that's the phrase?"

Roman nodded, and Wyatt started to laugh, the sound of it filling the room, jumping over to Roman, causing the two men to devolve into a fit of laughter. "This is insane," Wyatt said as his breath started coming back to him. "I don't even know what I'm laughing at. I just—this is wild. How am I sitting next to my high school freaking sweetheart, working on a job that could set us all up for life. How the hell?"

Roman chuckled, residual laughter bubbling up in his chest. He stretched his leg out, his knee grazing Wyatt's. "Life's crazy. One second, you're dreaming about someone, and the next, they're agreeing to come along on a heist of a lifetime."

"Is it really a heist? We're just collecting some pages, which—by the way—I still have no idea what they're about."

Roman smirked, having almost forgotten how blunt Wyatt could sometimes be. He liked it. Kept him on his toes. "We have to steal the book, which didn't exactly go great the first time we attempted it. This time, I guarantee the security will be increased, and the job is only going to be harder. Now, do you

The Sunset Job

have any other terminology issues you'd like to bring up?"

Wyatt shook his head. "Nope, nope. That sums it up pretty well." He hid his smile behind another drink, his lips coming back with a glitter of moisture to them, catching the dim lamplight that softened everything in the room. Wyatt's leg bounced slightly, causing it to rub against Roman's, sending lightning bolts racing up his thighs.

"High school sweetheart, huh?" Roman said, circling the conversation back.

"Well, yeah, we were inseparable. Was I not yours?"

"Of course you were. You were more than that, everything all at once. You were my happiest moments and my biggest regrets."

Wyatt's voice dropped. "What did you regret?"

"Not fighting tooth and nail for you. Letting you go, thinking it'd be best for you, only knowing that it would kill me. I should have listened to my heart. I should have chased after you, let you know how much I wanted you back at my side." Roman's throat grew tight, his head light. His heart started to hammer. Heat began to rise.

"How would you have let me know?" Wyatt asked, looking up into Roman's eyes.

Roman licked his lips. "Like this."

He went in, unable to hold anything back. His lips locked with Wyatt's, and they melted into one another, their tongues dancing and their breaths melding. Roman tasted the sweet berries from the wine, mixed with the taste unique only to Wyatt, one that exploded every single serotonin receptor in Roman's brain.

Roman's entire being became flooded with lust, his mind focusing on one thing and one thing only: getting Wyatt naked and underneath him. He pulled off Wyatt's shirt and tugged down his shorts, helped when Wyatt lifted himself off the couch. Wyatt's light blue briefs were doing a terrible job at holding in his erection. The pink head peeked from the side, already dripping wet.

Roman let out a hungry groan, rubbing Wyatt's stiffening length before getting down on his knees so that he could rub his face against him instead of his palm. "Jeez, Roman, you're so goddamn sexy. That feels so good."

He throbbed through the briefs, against Roman's cheek as he dug his nose into the crook of Wyatt's thigh, letting the precome wet the side of his face. He turned and ran his tongue over the leaking slit, earning a tortured moan from Wyatt, who now had a good grip on Roman's hair and was using it to tug him closer.

Roman pulled Wyatt's cock out from the leg of his briefs, admiring it for a moment before deciding he had to have it down his throat.

"Oh fuck," Wyatt hissed through a breath as his

hard cock stuffed Roman's mouth. Wyatt opened his legs a little wider and gripped Roman's head with both hands, pulling him down and holding him there, eyes rolling back with pleasure.

Roman gagged, coming up for air before licking his way down to Wyatt's balls, sucking one into his mouth and swirling his tongue, Wyatt's sweet, musky scent filling Roman with every deep inhale.

"Fuck, I missed this so fucking much," Roman said, stroking Wyatt and looking up into the most beautiful golden-brown eyes he'd ever seen, those symmetrical freckles contrasting the sinful gaze that poured from Wyatt's eyes.

It made Roman even hungrier, the craving to devour every piece of him intensifying.

"Take these off," Roman growled, standing up as he undressed in record time. Wyatt pulled off the blue briefs and threw them in the pile.

"There." Roman stepped forward, pulling Wyatt onto him. He clamped their lips together in a desperate kiss. A current of bliss coursed through him, originating from where their hard lengths crossed together, their shafts throbbing against the other. "God, you feel so good against me."

Wyatt nipped at Roman's neck. "Wait until you feel me on top of you."

"Yeah? You want to sit on my fat cock?"

"Mhmm," Wyatt whimpered as Roman reached around and grabbed a handful of his ass, his finger probing toward Wyatt's needy hole. Roman could feel the electricity buzzing through the man, sparks flying everywhere skin touched skin. A chemical reaction that threatened to blow more than just the roof off their hotel. They stumbled backward, toward a wall draped in red velvet. His toes sank into the plush carpet, curling downward as Wyatt thrust his hips forward, his cock painting Roman's belly with slick precome.

Roman brought his fingers up to Wyatt's mouth and let him suck on them, his tongue swirling around each one, popping it out and moving to the next with a lusty smile playing on his face. With his fingers coated in Wyatt's spit, he brought them back to Wyatt's tight hole, pushing forward and slipping in.

"Oh *fuuuuck*," Wyatt groaned as Roman went in further. His warm channel gave no resistance, the silky soft walls tightening around Roman. It drove him absolutely fucking wild, knowing that he was knuckle-deep inside of a man who had the ability to light his entire world on fire. A man who he'd been sure had gotten away, and one he never wanted to let go of again.

"Come," Roman said, walking them toward the bed, finger still inside of Wyatt. "I need to give you more than my finger."

Chapter 16

Wyatt Hernandez

WYATT'S BODY was being overrun with pleasure. Every single one of his circuits was misfiring, the sensation of Roman's finger inside of him was almost too much. He rolled his eyes back as they moved to the bed, where he got onto his fours and pushed his ass up. Roman curled his finger and pushed against Wyatt's swollen prostate, making his cock jerk and leak, a clear drop of precome falling down from the tip and wetting the silky-soft white sheets.

"Yeah, right there, Roman. Oh fuck, keep going. Yeah, add another finger, *ohhhhh* fuck." Wyatt dropped his head, arching his back as Roman stretched him open with two fingers. He heard him spit before feeling the warm and wet spread of his saliva, collecting it with his two fingers before pushing back in, pulling a gasp from deep in Wyatt's chest.

"Your ass is so fucking sexy. And tight. Fuck, Wyatt, I need you."

"You can have me. Whatever you want."

He started to slide his fingers in faster, harder, using his other hand to fondle Wyatt's tightening balls. More precome leaked down onto the sheets. He'd never been this wet before, had never seen such a dark stain underneath him, hadn't felt this kind of electricity in years. Not since... well, not since he and Roman had last been together.

Roman slipped his fingers out and gave Wyatt a chance to turn over onto his back. But Wyatt maneuvered himself so that he was lying with his head hanging off the bed, Roman's stiff cock lined up directly with his throat. Wyatt didn't even need to ask; he just opened his mouth, and Roman leaned forward, sliding his cock into Wyatt's waiting lips.

Instantly, Roman's taste exploded over Wyatt's senses.

"Oh fuck, baby." Roman softly rubbed both sides of Wyatt's face as he watched him swallow, Wyatt's lithe body stretched out on the bed, his own dick twitching in the air.

Roman reached forward, moving past Wyatt's needy cock and finding his hole again. He found no resistance as he pushed back in, Wyatt's body greedily accepting him. He palmed at Wyatt's balls while his fingers went back to massaging that spongy spot that worked the same for every man—the equivalent of pushing a big red nuclear button.

Wyatt continued to suck him off, his toes curling into the bed as he ground his ass down on Roman's hand. This was what he wanted, all he ever wanted. He likely wouldn't admit that when his brain wasn't so addled with cock and balls, but in this moment, he could see it clear as a summer's day in LA: he wanted Roman, and he had never *stopped* wanting him. No matter what the man did to ruin his life, Wyatt had missed him, missed this.

It was an undeniable feeling of *life*, warm and golden and glittery and rare.

And he didn't want to let it go. Not again.

"Fuck me," Wyatt said, Roman's thick cock resting gently against his cheek. He buried his nose between the crook of the man's balls and thigh, breathing in his sweet, earthy scent. "Please, Roman. Fuck me."

Roman pulled his fingers out, leaving Wyatt even more ravaged for his cock. Thankfully, he didn't have to wait much longer. Roman went over to his suitcase and took out a small bottle of lube, Wyatt moving so that he was lying down properly on the bed, his head against the grand headboard. The red velvet curtains that could be draped around the canopy bed were instead held up with thick golden ropes, matching the gold of the four posts.

Wyatt felt like royalty, watching his king walk

back in the dim lamplight, his six-pack rippling with every step, the old-school tattoo of a traditionally drawn snake and blade sitting in the center of his chest, the perfect amount of flowers surrounding it.

Wyatt could have come right then and there but somehow managed to hold on.

"I've been tested," Roman said, "and I'm on PrEP."

"I know my status, too: negative. I think we're good without condoms." Wyatt practically drooled as Roman climbed onto the bed, hard cock waving in the air. "Go slow," he warned as Roman lined himself up, grabbing both of Wyatt's legs and lifting them up for easier access.

"Of course. You tell me if I need to stop." He kissed the inside of Wyatt's leg, lips soft against his skin. Wyatt dropped his head back and relaxed, trusting in Roman, opening himself up for him.

Roman did go slow, pushing forward inch by orgasmic inch. Wyatt's body stretched to accommodate him, burning but only in the best way, and only momentarily. Soon, the burn gave way to the pleasure, flames licking up Wyatt's side as Roman sank into him completely, their eyes locked and their faces twisting with ecstasy.

"That okay?" Roman asked, kissing Wyatt's other calf, cock throbbing inside of him.

"Yes, fuck, you're so big. Hold on." Wyatt looked down, his own length twitching in the air, Roman's abs shifting with every breath as they remained locked together. The flames grew hotter, the room catching with it, the temperature skyrocketing.

"Go, harder."

Roman nodded, shifting his hips backward before plunging forward again. And again.

And again and again.

"Oh fuck, yes, Roman, fuck, keep going. Harder, harder. Yes, ohhhh—" Wyatt's words were throttled by a savage kiss, matching the intensity of Roman's thrusts. He reached up and latched onto Roman's shoulders, nails digging into skin, pain mixing with pleasure mixing with bliss mixing with primal lust. Nothing mattered, nothing but the slapping of skin against skin, the union of two men trying to reach their ultimate peaks.

"Yes, yes, oh shit, Roman, baby, you're going to make me come."

"Do it," he growled, fucking into Wyatt so that it echoed in the room. "Blow your load. I want to feel your ass when you come."

Wyatt's eyebrows dipped, his mouth forming the shape of an O and losing all ability to form words. His entire body gave a spasm as Roman fucked the come right out of him, Wyatt shooting jets of come right over his shoulder, splattering the headboard, some of it landing on his chin.

Roman's grunts turned animalistic, his thrusts erratic. His eyes rolled back as he came, filling Wyatt up, so much so that Wyatt could feel the streams of come.

Both of them, spent and emptied, melted into the bed, Roman's entire body weight creating a comforting pressure.

The blissful mix of oxytocin and endorphins flooded Wyatt and turned him into a giddy blob of a human. He chuckled into Roman's chest, only just beginning to get feeling back in his toes, the rest of his nervous system catching up after the hard restart Roman had just given him. He reached over and managed to grab a shirt, wiping himself off as best he could.

"Goddamn," Roman said, kissing Wyatt's head, his swollen cock still plugging Wyatt. "I think I lost my vision there for a second."

"And I think I died for a second. Like I saw the other side. Holy shit."

Roman laughed, his body encasing Wyatt's, surrounding him in a sense of peace and safety. Roman shifted his hips and pulled himself out, leaving Wyatt slightly sore and already craving more, come dripping down the back of his thigh. He flipped over, throwing a leg over Roman's, both of them looking up at the ceiling with drunken smiles playing on their dimly lit faces.

"When did you learn how to move your ass like that?" Roman asked as he moved an arm underneath Wyatt, who cuddled in with his head resting on

The Sunset Job

Roman's smooth, muscular chest.

"You haven't been the only one living life these past few years. I've managed to have a good time, even without you around."

"As good a time as you had tonight?"

Wyatt mulled that one over for a second. "No, not as good as tonight."

Roman smiled, twirling Wyatt's messy hair between two fingers. It was one of Wyatt's favorite displays of affection, whenever someone would lazily stroke his head, playing with his hair and massaging his scalp.

"What did you mean, back in the underwater tunnel? How you've been through some shit? What happened, Roman?"

His chest rose with a deep breath, lifting Wyatt's head with it. He could hear the woosh of air that filled his lungs. The *lub-dub* beat of his heart, slow and rhythmic. All of Roman's inner workings creating a soundtrack of Wyatt's most loved music.

"A lot happened, more than I think I can say in a night."

"What's the biggest thing that happened, then? Since I've been gone?"

Another deep breath filled his chest. "Well, let's see. I ended up graduating but got mixed up with the wrong people, my uncle being one of them. He brought me into his 'business' after I graduated, and I helped him for a couple of years, watching him lead and learning as I went along. Three years into it, and we were betrayed. An entire job ended up being a trap, and we walked right into it."

"Who set the trap?"

"The Pride. Leonidas himself. He hated my uncle, always said it was because of my uncle stealing his wife, but I had a feeling it ran even deeper than that. Leonidas executed him, right in front of me. I was next, but Mimic—she was part of my uncle's original crew—she was there and saved the day.

"I changed after that. I'd never taken a life before then, always using blunt force to knock someone out or aiming for nonvitals if I had to shoot. After that, my aim shifted. Pulling the trigger became easier, but so did becoming a leader. I slipped right into the role, and over time, I collected the group we have today."

"The Rainbow's Seven," Wyatt said, his fingers trailing down Roman's side.

"You know, the day before my uncle died, I had a dream. It was one I had often, but I remember it being so fucking vivid that night. It was you and me, lying out on a beach, but the ocean was full of stars instead of water. And we'd make love until the sun disappeared and reappeared at least twice, three, four, five times. Lost track, until I'd wake up. It was one of those dreams that leave you depressed the second you open your eyes and realize none of it was real.

"I wanted to make it real. I booked a flight—I still

have it in my email. I was going to find you, apologize for everything. Make it right somehow. Except I never made the flight."

Wyatt opened his mouth but couldn't really find the words to respond. He'd gone on thinking that Roman never tried to get back with him, that he never even wanted to apologize for the shit he put Wyatt through. But that wasn't entirely the case. Life appeared to have other plans, and the timing wasn't exactly perfect, but Roman found his way back into Wyatt's orbit, apology in hand.

"It worked out the way it was meant to," Wyatt said, managing to let go of the bitter, cold grudge he held on to after all those years. Yes, there was shit in their past that he wished had never happened, but none of that mattered much anymore. They were back, together, and they had a job to finish. What happened after that was still up in the air, but Wyatt wasn't so scared of it anymore. Being here felt right, as much as he resisted the idea initially.

Roman felt right.

"Don't hurt me again, okay?"

"I won't," Roman answered, kissing Wyatt's forehead before wrapping his arm around him a little tighter. Wyatt leaned over him and turned the bedside lamp off, plunging them into a room only lit by moonlight, pearlescent and dreamy. Wyatt settled in, the mattress forming a cloud underneath him, eyelids growing heavy.

"Promise?" Wyatt asked, his heart slightly settled but brain far from it.

"I swear it. I've got your back, Salt. No matter what happens, I've got you. And I'm never letting you go."

Wyatt accepted that answer as fully fact, a smile forming on his lips, Roman's body heat creating a deliciously warm cocoon around him. His eyelids became even heavier, matching the weight in his useless limbs. He wanted to ask another question, wanted to stay up until they had to board their plane to Paris the next morning. He wanted to keep re-exploring every inch of Roman's body before the night was up.

It only took seventy-three seconds of silence for sleep to take them, the two men drifting into dreams featuring both as the main stars, an ocean of twinkling lights as the backdrop.

Chapter 17

Roman Ashford

THE SUN BEAT down on Roman as he lay back on the lawn chair, looking out at the Seine and drinking a cold beer. They were at the north bank of the river, famous for being turned into the Paris Plage for summer: Paris Beach. Blue beach umbrellas lined the bank, where Parisians and tourists alike came to drink and hang out, creating the perfect place to watch the sunset over one of the famous bridges or the Notre Dame, its facade being reconstructed but still offering a stunning view. Behind them was a sand volleyball court, where Bang Bang, Phantom, and Wyatt were playing against Mimic, Mustang, and Doc. Loud music from the nearby bars drifted over the general chatter and laughter of the gathered crowd.

It scared Roman how well things seemed to be going, *especially* after this morning when he woke up with a naked Wyatt wrapped in his arms and realizing none of it had been a dream. It was all real, and *that's* what terrified him. He couldn't shake the feeling that he was standing on a rug and it was slowly inching out from under him, ready to get yanked completely at any moment.

That sensation wasn't helped at all by the fact that there could be a traitor in the midst. He hated to think about it but knew that his primary job as the leader of this crew was to keep everyone safe. If one of their own was working with the Pride, telegraphing their moves and helping them out... that would have to be handled.

But who? He trusted each of those six people with his own life, and all for different reasons. Yes, money talked, and if the Pride was offering some kind of ludicrous sum for information, he could see how some people might flip, but not anyone in his Rainbow's Seven. Especially not with the job they were on. If they made it to the end, all seven of them would have over half a billion dollars in untraceable money.

This was their sunset job, the final one, where the reward would allow them each to sail off on their own private yachts and into their own personal paradise.

So maybe it wasn't money. Maybe there was another link? Some other connection that was overriding the bond between the crew.

The Sunset Job

But what? And who?

Roman leaned back in the chair and looked up at the sky, tossing around impossible-sounding possibilities. Mimic—who'd had his back since they met on a hijacked bus in Brazil after a job went wrong—would never betray him, unless there was something he was missing. Maybe something to do with her mother? She lived off-grid near Pride territory, having been married to one of them, making Mimic a stepdaughter to the criminal organization hot on their tail.

Bang Bang? The big, burly, trigger-happy (and overall just *happy*) bear of a man who Roman considered to be his best friend, but was that title enough to stop him from taking some kind of outrageous offer in exchange for information? Bang Bang loved his guns and collected rare ones, going to great lengths to acquire a few of them. Could the Pride have something he wanted badly enough to screw over the Rainbow's Seven?

Phantom, Mustang, Doc... Wyatt. He couldn't imagine any of them stabbing him in the back. And it was in those blind spots that mistakes were made.

"You need more sunscreen," Doc said, sitting down in a chair, tying her hair up in a loose ponytail. She tossed over the bright orange bottle of sunscreen, and Roman caught it with one hand. "Your forehead is starting to look like a baboon's asshole."

Roman gave a hearty laugh at that imagery. "Is it the baboon's asshole that's red or the butt cheeks?"

Doc tilted her head and pushed out her bottom lip. "That—hmm, that's a good question. Too bad I'm a trained medical professional and not a zoologist specializing in primate assholes."

"Who's an asshole?" Bang Bang said, dropping into a chair, the rest of the gang coming up behind him.

"No one, we're just talking about monkeys." Roman stood up, looking around at the assembled group, sweaty and sandy after their game. "But enough about baboons and their assholes. We've got work to do today."

Phantom arched a brow. "Baboon... assholes?"

Doc nodded and asked, "Yeah, do you think they're red or skin colored?"

"Damn, you know, I've never really thought of—"

"Yeah, none of us have, Phantom. We'll figure it out later. Google it if you want, just make sure you have private browsing set up." Roman gave Doc a wink before she rolled her eyes and grabbed her phone, her sparkly fuchsia nails flying across the screen.

"Alright, now that you guys are warmed up, I think it's time to go get what we came for. Everyone clear on the plan?"

They all nodded. It wasn't a very complicated plan to begin with, and it would only kick in if the

The Sunset Job

phrase Roman was given didn't work for whatever reason. He was done getting surprised, so having a plan B this leg of the job was crucial.

Roman would go in first, find Amelie, and say the phrase he was told to say. If all went right, he'd be handed the page, and off they went on their merry way, one step closer to billions of dollars.

If that didn't work, then plan B went into effect. Mimic, Bang Bang, and Wyatt would go into the bakery under the guise of husbands accompanied by their wedding planner, looking for lavish cakes for their big gay wedding. While they distracted Amelie downstairs, Phantom would sneak past and break into her upstairs apartment. He'd have thirty minutes tops to case the place and find the page before Amelie grew suspicious of her new customers.

"Doc and Mustang, you guys can drive ahead. Scout the place out and make sure none of those Pride fuckers are around. We'll walk over there. It shouldn't be far."

Mustang smiled, pushing some rogue curls out of her face. "I'll race you there."

"I think it's safe to say you'll win that one."

"I'll pop a tire. Give you all an advantage. Not a big one, mind you."

Roman smirked, a hand on Mustang's shoulder, answering with a simple "Fuck no."

Mustang laughed and left with Doc, the two of them teasing each other about their big loss in the volleyball match, Doc blaming it on the fact that Mustang couldn't keep her eyes off Mimic.

"What about you and Bang Bang?" Mustang asked. "He almost spiked the ball into your gaping jaws. Probably wished it was something else."

That was the last the crew heard of them before they got into the car. Bang Bang looked around, grinning from ear to ear. "She was checking me out, huh?"

They started down the packed river bank, friends and families and couples all basking in the sun, soaking in all of the energy that the most romantic city on this planet had to offer. You could feel it in the air—a magic in the warmth, a sparkle in the light, a shine in everyone's eyes. Couples leaned over picnic baskets and laughed through their kisses, hands touching, wineglasses empty.

"This place is beautiful. It's like all the stories say —Paris really is the city of love," Wyatt said at his side, plucking the thoughts right out of his own head. "I can't believe I'm even here."

"I'm glad you are," Roman said, and his belly suddenly did a summersault through a field of butterflies as he reached for Wyatt's hand. He had an urge and decided to act on it, hoping it wasn't a dumb move. Wyatt stiffened for the slightest moment, his eyes looking ahead at Phantom, Mimic, and Bang Bang arguing about the best flavor macarons they'd had.

Wyatt didn't pull away, though. He did the opposite and opened his fingers, allowing Roman's to slip through.

"Remember that one time in high school French?" Roman asked as memories flooded back, like a dam had broken. "When Mrs. Bodin caught us making out under the desk?"

Wyatt laughed, his smile brighter than the sunshine. "And you told her that we were just practicing our French kiss."

"Fucking ridiculous. God, kids are terrible." Roman matched Wyatt's belly laughs.

"Atrocious, monstrous. They scare me, and I work at a science museum with daily field trips, so you can imagine the horrors I've seen and heard."

"*Worked*," Roman corrected. "After this, you'll be able to buy out the Science Museum and turn it into a leather bar or something."

"That'd be a big-ass leather bar."

Roman shrugged. "Is that a problem?"

"Not at all, no. I don't mind a harness or two." Wyatt smirked, lighting a fuse deep in Roman's core. Heat spread from where their hands met, climbing up his arm, down his chest, trailing his abs and settling in his balls.

Fuck, I can't wait to get him back in our hotel room. We're not sleeping tonight.

"Maybe I can call it The Throat Goat?" Wyatt mused.

"The Throat what?"

"Throat G.O.A.T.: The throat that's the greatest of all time. At, well, you know." Wyatt pressed his tongue against his cheek, creating a familiar-looking bulge.

Roman laughed, nodding his head as he filed away the new vocabulary. "I think that can work," he said. "Definitely inspired by the owner."

Wyatt cocked his head with a smile playing on his lips.

They turned onto a tight street full of tourists window-shopping the various boutiques. Ahead of them was the Eiffel Tower, framed by the Romeo and Juliet balconies that adorned the row of buildings on either side of them. Roman and Wyatt separated as the crowd grew thicker, people filing between them with their eyes on their phones, trying to capture the perfect shot of the Eiffel Tower, likely already taken about a thousand times today alone.

A couple of streets over, they found themselves in front of Amelie's bakery, its storefront displaying a decedent assortment of sweets through the glass: buttery scones that glittered with powdered sugar, red velvet cupcakes next to a shining mango tart, and an assortment of blueberry croissants that looked unreal. A stand full of colorful macarons was arranged to resemble a rainbow. The scent of fresh-baked goods wafted through the open door as smiling customers walked out with a bag full of baguettes.

The Sunset Job

"Buy me a chocolate croissant," Bang Bang said before Roman entered the store. "Actually, get me three."

Roman gave him a thumbs-up and entered, immediately spotting Amelie behind the counter, chatting with a customer as if they were old friends. She looked up and said a cheerful "Bonjour" in Roman's direction, which he returned. He made himself busy looking over a refrigerated case of the most elaborate and detailed cakes he'd ever seen. The piping alone must have taken days with some of them, designs with perfect filigree flowing around three tiers of smooth white icing, a stunning collection of frosting roses and tulips sitting on top like an actual flower crown. Roman could see how she had earned her title as one of the most creative and expert bakers in all of France.

The customer grabbed his box of macarons and hugged Amelie over the counter. She turned toward the back room, leaving her employees to take care of the front, mentioning something about an alert in her security system. Except none of them could handle Roman's request, so before she disappeared to the back, he shouted out for her, "Bonjour, Amelie."

She stopped, one hand on the door. Her apron was covered in flour, some of it dusting the strands of her long black hair. She cocked her head and offered Roman a smile. "I'm so sorry, sir, do I know you?"

"No, you don't. But I knew your son."

Her hand dropped from the door, and a wrinkle appeared between her eyebrows.

This was it, the moment of truth. She either had the page and recognized the phrase, or she didn't, and this job would become a whole lot more complicated. Her son had mentioned that she kept the page in her home above the bakery, but what if she didn't understand the importance of it? What if she got rid of it? Forgot the phrase?

Thankfully, Roman didn't have to wait long at all to get his answers.

Here goes nothing.

"Listen to the blue jays sing," Roman said, hoping to all hope he wasn't just saying this to sound dumb. "It's like paradise."

Her eyes widened with fear, and her skin blanched. She walked backward toward the door and nearly shouted her next words.

"Get out. Go!"

Chapter 18

Wyatt Hernandez

Wyatt looked at his watch. Ten minutes had passed, longer than he thought it'd take to either get the page or figure out she didn't have it. They were seated around a bistro table, the white-and-blue weaving fabric matching those of the chairs. Phantom cracked his knuckles and moved to stand but didn't make it off his seat before Roman walked out of the door, a cheery bell ringing over his head in contrast to the dark storm that clouded his expression.

It was clear to Wyatt that he didn't get the page. Even though years separated much of their relationship, he could still read the emerald-eyed man like his favorite book, spine worn and pages dog-eared.

"You guys are up," Roman said, pulling out a bistro chair and sitting down. "She flipped when I said the phrase."

"What, why? What happened in there?" Mimic asked. She wore a short blonde wig that had silver streaks through it, wearing fake turquoise glasses that matched with her slightly gaudy turquoise necklace. Wyatt had only known her for a short amount of time but still managed to be struck by how easily she could transform herself, this artsy and slightly kooky wedding planner worlds away from the raven-haired and effortlessly stylish Mimic who carried herself like a resurrected queen.

"Someone was here already. She said he came late last night and told her the phrase but that it was off by a few words. When she wouldn't give him the page, he pulled out a knife on her and tried to take it by force. A pair of police were walking by the bakery just then, and he got scared, ran off.

"She told me that she'll be destroying the page tonight, that she doesn't want anything else to do with it or her dead son's games."

"Damn it," Phantom said. "Not great."

"And it gets worse."

Wyatt sat up, unsure of what else could go wrong.

"She said that the man wore a necklace with some kind of claw hanging off the end. The Pride's been here."

Bang Bang dropped his head into those big bear paws of his, a collection of different rings shining on his fingers. Phantom let out a high-pitched whistle.

The Sunset Job

"Yeah," Roman said. "My feelings exactly. Thankfully, they weren't able to get the page, so we've got that going for us. Now it's up to you three. Good luck." He reached under the table and squeezed Wyatt's knee. The physical contact in front of the others may have unsettled Wyatt earlier on in this adventure of theirs, but he was beginning to warm up to it. Want it. Give it back in return.

He put his hand on Roman's and squeezed. A way to tell him "he had this" even though he wasn't entirely sure he did. Flashes of their last gunfight in the midst of the Spanish elite came rushing back in, creating a tremble in his shoulders that he worked hard to suppress.

"Ready, boys?" Mimic asked.

Bang Bang and Phantom both nodded, Bang Bang reaching across the table for Wyatt's hand and shooting him a wink. "Let's go, hubby."

"You're not hubbies just yet," Roman reminded him, a sliver of something resembling jealousy narrowing his eyes. It quickly faded, replaced by a glint that was enhanced with his growing smile. "Don't forget your chocolate croissants. I wasn't able to get them."

"Yeah, I know," Bang Bang said with an eye roll. The three of them stood and walked into the store, the door closing just enough for Phantom to slip in behind them without the bell ringing.

Wyatt was instantly impressed (and hungry) at

seeing the assortment of baked goods, all made as if they were plucked straight from the cover of a food magazine. The displays were bordered with gold that matched the gold ceiling. Mimic walked the two hand-holding men—Wyatt's smaller hand getting lost in Bang Bang's—directly to the counter, where she spoke in fluent French to the smiley guy in a flour-dusted apron. She explained to him that her clients came from two very influential political families and their wedding was set to be a grand affair, except it was also on very short notice. She needed to speak with Amelie about making a cake under a very tight timeline.

There was some pushback from the man, his smile slowly fading as Mimic persisted. Wyatt couldn't understand a lick of what they were saying, but he could read body language, and the story that was being told with stiffening shoulders and tightening lips wasn't a good one.

He took that moment to look around the store again. There were a couple of framed photos showing the opening of the bakery, along with her standing in front of another location, pointing up to the name of the bakery: Remy's Sweet Treats. It was a nicely arranged set of photos with a tray of sugar-dusted pastries in front of it. He took a picture, wanting to have some photographic evidence of all the cool places he'd been to. Julie would want to see it when he got back home; she loved going through travel photos with him.

The pretty frames and mouthwatering tarts weren't all Wyatt noticed.

Phantom's gone.

The ghost must have already walked through the walls. Wyatt wasn't sure how, considering that the entrance to Amelie's upstairs apartment was in plain view of the entire store, but he was grateful nonetheless. The sooner Phantom got up there and dug around, the quicker they could grab the page and get the hell out of there.

"Merci," Mimic said, crossing her arms and tugging at her necklace in a nervous tic that must have been birthed for this character. "He's going to go get her." She shot a glance at the clock sitting above a basket of freshly baked baguettes. "We've got about twenty-five minutes."

The two swinging doors behind the counter opened, Amelie wiping her hands on her beige apron. There was a designer quality to it in the delicate embroidery that went up the sides, only seen under perfect lighting, the ivory strap around her neck appearing soft as silk and durable as cotton.

Her expression wasn't nearly as soft, something clearly having upset her.

"Bonjour," she said, walking around the counter and shaking both Bang Bang's and Wyatt's hands.

"Laurent explained to me all about your wedding and how important this is to both of you. I do want to be honest with you, eh, today has not been the best. I'm a little all over the place, but considering the timeline—"

"So sorry about the inconvenience," Mimic said, jumping in. "Truly, if we could rewind time a bit, we would. Unfortunately, we can't."

Amelie wrung her hands before sliding them into the pockets of her dress, some of the flour having made its way onto the light blue-and-yellow floral pattern. "I understand, and by no means do I want to be the reason for any delays. Come, let's go to my office, and we can talk cake. Is that okay?"

"Yes, perfect," Wyatt said, offering a smile that may have been a little *too* stretched. He leaned into Bang Bang, trying to sell the fantasy as best he could.

"Great, let me just go upstairs to grab my office keys."

"Actually—" all three spoke at the same time, Bang Bang's loud voice carrying over all of them. "We can talk about cakes out here. We really like vanilla and chocolate, especially chocolate. Right, Peter?"

Wyatt felt an instinctual push to ignore the question. His name wasn't Peter, after all.

But his cover name certainly was. "Yup, chocolate and vanilla. We're pretty basic."

"Well, we can work with that. I have some really wonderful marble cakes that I can decorate any way

The Sunset Job

you'd like. Let me just get the photo album inside my office, that way you can see what I have made before."

"There's really no need for that, Amelie," Mimic said, reaching over a hand heavy with a brass ring holding a turquoise stone. "We've seen all your incredible work online already. Really very magical. My clients usually don't have the budget for your skill, if I'm honest, but I'm glad Peter and Francisco can have your magic at their wedding."

That seemed to soften her up some, a shaky smile forming on her face, cheekbones fragile and angular, highlighted by a natural blush that filled her cheeks. "That is very special to hear, thank you... Okay, let's look at the cakes we have on display, then. That should give you an idea of what we can do."

"Excellent," Wyatt said, Bang Bang repeating him. They walked over to the assortment of cakes displayed behind a brightly lit glass, covered in smooth fondant and icing of all different colors and designs. There were flower-filled cakes and fruit-covered cakes and chocolate-drizzled cakes, strawberry and red velvet and orange.

"And how long have you two been together?"

"Three years," Bang Bang said.

"Two years," Wyatt said before catching himself and laughing. "I'm terrible with remembering that kind of stuff. Three years, that's right."

Amelie nodded, taking out a few plates and forks

for tasting. Wyatt checked the time again, hoping to hear Phantom's voice buzzing in through the earpiece at any moment, telling the team that he got what they came for.

"Okay, shall we start with the straw—sorry, that's my alarm system buzzing." She pulled out her phone, and Wyatt could feel his heart stop beating. Was there something they overlooked, a security system Wyatt hadn't turned off before they got there? He'd been in charge of taking down the cameras and alarms, all of which was quite easy after connecting to her own computer through her Wi-Fi.

A heavy crash rattled the ceiling, coming from directly above them. Another crash and then a loud bang followed.

"What in the world?" Amelie craned her neck and looked upward, same as the rest of them.

Except for Bang Bang. He ran toward the door leading upstairs, leaping over the counter, causing a couple of browsing customers to gasp in shock. That was when Phantom's voice echoed inside Wyatt's skull, carrying with it devastating news, far from the fantasy Wyatt had whipped up earlier when he was imagining this all going as smooth as the icing on the cakes.

"I've been shot," Phantom said, breathless. "I need help."

Chapter 19

Roman Ashford

Roman didn't need to wait for confirmation to know what he'd just heard was a gunshot. He jumped up from the chair, sending it falling to the floor as he dashed to the door. A couple sipping on their coffees looked at Roman like he was crazy, one even rolling their eyes as Roman disappeared into the bakery.

"Where are you, Phantom?" he asked into the earpiece, looking for Wyatt and seeing him run through a set of double doors with Mimic next to him.

Fuck.

He wanted to keep Wyatt far from this mess, but it looked like Salt had a different idea, and he ran after them. An apron-wearing clerk was crouched behind the counter with his hands over his head, fear in his big brown eyes. "Go outside, hurry."

The scared man nodded, Roman's words cutting through the haze of adrenaline. He got to his feet and bolted in the opposite direction as Roman, the bell chiming behind him as he ran into the street shouting for help.

The double doors opened into a hallway lit by a row of fluorescent bulbs.

"Upstairs, living room. There's two guys up here. Be careful."

More gunshots rattled through the building. Roman took the staircase three steps at a time, unholstering his gun and clicking off the safety. The stairs left him in a small circular room, the door to Amelie's apartment directly in front of him, thrown off its hinges.

Definitely not Phantom's work.

Roman ran to the wall, pressing his back against it. He peeked over and spotted Wyatt and Mimic crouched behind a couch, Wyatt holding down a bundled-up T-shirt soaked with blood against Phantom's wound. Meanwhile, Bang Bang stood in the center of the room framed by a window that looked out directly to the Eiffel Tower, both arms held out and raised, golden guns aimed at two Pride members. They *also* had their arms up and their guns aimed, outnumbering Bang Bang two to one.

This was bad, but it could be worse.

Bang Bang could take the shots and drop both men instantly, Roman was positive of that. He had full confidence in his best friend, knew that he could save the day. Even with being outnumbered. Bang Bang worked best under pressure, and this was pressure at its most extreme.

What Roman wasn't counting on was Amelie trying to save the day herself. She jumped onto the back of one of the Pride men like a rabid cat, latching onto his shoulders and tugging at his hair, trying to drop him to the ground. It made it impossible for Bang Bang to shoot without potentially hitting her.

The distraction created an opening, the other man dropping to his knees and letting go of his gun, taking out a serrated blade from the inside of his boot, rolling forward.

He launched up, the blade aimed directly at Bang Bang's throat. The man moved too quick, fluid in a way that appeared otherworldly. He rose like a vine ready to choke the life out of Bang Bang.

Roman wasn't letting that happen. He lurched out of cover and took less than a second to aim, time slowing, stretching, his muscles taut as high wire, his eyesight sharp as a hawk's.

He pulled the trigger. *Bang.*

Thud.

The man dropped like a bag of lead at Bang Bang's feet.

Bang Bang gave Roman a wink and shouted, "Thank you," before turning both golden pistols in the other man's direction, Amelie still clinging to his back like a spider monkey.

"Drop and run," Roman shouted, but Amelie wasn't listening. She was reaching over the man's shoulders to try and grab the gun. What the hell had gotten into her? "Drop!"

That seemed to cut through the chaos. She lifted her head and looked to Roman, eyes widening with fear as she realized the immense danger she was actually in. She fell to the ground. The man turned and kicked her, causing her to clutch at her stomach. He shouted profanities but kept the gun aimed at Bang Bang.

"Do you want to walk out of here in one piece?" Roman asked, taking a step forward. From the corner of his eye, he could see Wyatt trying to keep Phantom awake, slapping his face. The T-shirt pressed against his chest was soaked with blood. It didn't look good. Roman knew he had to finish this quick if he wanted to get everyone out of here alive. "Then drop the fucking gun and run. Tell Leonidas what happened. Let him know this shit won't be easy for him."

The man's eyes narrowed to slits. He lowered his gun and glanced at the door. Roman was giving this fucker a lifeline; would he take it? Make everyone's life just that much easier? His eyes darted down to his dead buddy, blood still leaking from the hole in his chest.

The Sunset Job

"I've got a better idea," the man said, a heavy Italian accent coloring his words. He spun around and grabbed Amelie. She tried to run but wasn't fast enough, the man grabbing her apron strings and yanking her backward into his arms. He pressed the gun against her head.

"I'm going to get the page, and I'm going to make my boss happy. Now, where is it?" He held Amelie against him, crouching behind her so her body served as a shield. "Where is it!"

"It's not even in here," Amelie said, loud enough to make the entire room freeze. "I moved it! It isn't here—it's with my son. You won't find it. You won't."

"So you're telling me you're useless?"

Roman's eyes widened. Bang Bang moved to his side, all three guns aimed at a terrified Amelie.

"I... I won't tell you where it is."

"Fine," the man said. "Waste of time this was."

Roman looked up, a dangling light fixture directly above them. If he could hit the chain that connected it to the ceiling, maybe he could cause a distraction big enough to save Amelie. He only had seconds to think, to weigh out his actions.

He took the shot, raising his gun and pulling the trigger. The bullet rocketed up toward the light fixture, skimming the chain and tearing through the ceiling, plaster and wood falling down where the light fixture should have been.

Roman missed.

Another shot blasted through the air, and Amelie cried out and fell. The man leaped to the side, jumping through a window. Bang Bang tried getting him, but he was too fast, already disappearing in the alley behind the bakery. Roman went straight to Amelie, turning her over, blood trickling down her mouth, her gaze empty of life. She was gone.

He dropped his head and whispered a "sorry" before closing her eyes and laying her gently onto the floor. This wasn't how it was supposed to go. *Fuck.* Another leg of this job completely rat-fucked. Had it been a coincidence that the Pride was here at the same time they were?

In this business, Roman rarely believed in coincidences. Still—it didn't really matter, not right then. He knew his next steps were to get Phantom safe and stabilized. He wasn't losing anyone else today.

"Mustang, pull up the van. Doc, get ready to treat a gunshot wound."

He ran over to the couch, squeezing a reassuring hand around Wyatt's, his entire arm covered in blood.

It was worse than he thought. "Phantom, buddy, you're okay. We've got you. Just stay with us, alright? Doc is going to make you feel brand-new."

"Maybe she'll even throw in a new nose or a little tuck under the chin for you, free of charge," Bang Bang teased.

Phantom, whose normally bright honey-gold eyes

appeared to be having trouble focusing, smiled. Roman took over applying pressure. He noticed Wyatt's shoulders were trembling, but his face was stoic, courageous. Even with one of their own bleeding out on the floor, Wyatt still managed to hold his composure.

Proud didn't even begin to cut it.

"Help me with his legs," Roman said to Bang Bang. He motioned at the bloodied T-shirt. "Mimic, keep the pressure on while we move him. Salt, grab the doors."

They moved like they shared one mind, keeping things as smooth as possible for Phantom. Every second mattered, though, so they couldn't be too delicate. They hurried down the stairs and through the bakery, leaving a trail of blood behind them. Mustang waited outside, her eyes bulging when she saw the shape Phantom was in.

Doc waited in the back of the van, having already set up a space to work, a thin cushion placed for Phantom. They put him down gently and climbed in, Roman shutting the doors and Mustang peeling off as the police sirens grew louder.

"What the fuck happened in there?" Mustang shouted over the sound of the engine protesting.

Roman didn't have an answer for her. He didn't know. Once again, he'd led his own into the jaws of an ambush predator, the trap having been set without him picking up a whiff of it. And for what? They didn't even have the page, nor did they know where it was.

"Hold this," Doc said to Wyatt, handing him a suture set before she moved off the towel and examined the wound. She worked with the focus of a brain surgeon, her hands somehow staying steady even with the rattle of the racing van. She went into her indigo toolkit, grabbing a syringe and popping the cap off with her teeth. She injected the pain medicine into Phantom's forearm, his expression instantly softening with the relief. She gently rubbed his forehead and whispered something in his ear.

"Is he going to be okay?" Wyatt asked, unable to keep the tremble from entering his voice.

"It's a clean wound, entrance and exit. I'm scared with the amount of bleeding but have ways to help that." She took out a pack of green and red herbs from the toolbox and set it gently against Phantom's lips. "Chew on this," she said before grabbing the suture kit from Wyatt.

"Should I tell Mustang to slow down?" Roman asked.

She shook her head. "No need. She can go faster if she likes." And Doc got to work, suturing Phantom shut while the crew looked on, Roman plagued with thoughts of doubt, of anger, of "what the hell was this all for?"

Chapter 20

Wyatt Hernandez

WYATT WATCHED in stunned silence as Doc took care of Phantom, being as delicate as if she were handling a budding flower, the sharp turns and rattling van doing nothing to break her concentration and focus. She used her hands in the way a magician would, seemingly pulling salves and sutures out of thin air, all while uttering gentle reassurances and keeping her patient as calm as possible. Next to her was a bundle of bloodied cloths, some of them having been used to wash off the blood from Wyatt's hands.

Bang Bang craned his neck from the passenger seat. "How's he doing back there?"

"Good," Roman said. "Stable and awake."

"Here, give him some of this." Bang Bang pulled out a rose-gold flask from his pocket and reached it over. Wyatt grabbed it, uncapping the flask and taking a whiff.

"Smells like good rum," Wyatt said over the sound of tires spinning over rocks and gravel. He held the flask up against Phantom's lips.

"It's damn good rum, *broki*. Directly from my family's farm in Puerto Rico."

"Thanks," Phantom said, lifting a hand and wiping his smiling lips, seemingly unaware of the antibiotics being injected into his arm.

"Mind if I take a sip?" Wyatt asked before handing back the flask.

"Of course, *broki*. Take it home."

Wyatt didn't finish it, but he did take a sip and was pleasantly surprised at just how good the warm, golden drink tasted. He was normally a whiskey kind of guy, but Bang Bang's family rum may have just switched him over. He took another sip before seeing if Roman wanted some. He shook his head and continued to look out the tinted windows, the city of Paris blurring past in a way that erased all the romance.

"We fucked up," Roman said. They were sat on the floor of the van's rear, cross-legged with their backs against the uncomfortable plastic protrusion where the wheel was housed. "The Pride wasn't up there looking for the page—they were waiting to attack. They knew. And now one of ours is hurt, and we don't have the page."

"Amelie didn't even have the page," Wyatt noted, as if that would help.

The Sunset Job

"And it's not like we can exactly call her and ask where she hid it."

"No, no we can't." A particularly bumpy stretch of road had Wyatt falling against Roman. He put a hand on Roman's thigh to stabilize himself but didn't take it away once the road flattened out. "She did say something pretty interesting. How it's with her son."

"Which doesn't make much sense, unless she dug up his gravesite and dropped the page inside."

Wyatt shook his head. "She doesn't seem like the type of person who'd do that." And that's when it hit him, like a comet hurtling out of the sky. He dug in his pockets and pulled out his phone, scrolling directly to his photo album. "She *does* seem like the type to name her new bakery after her son, though."

He tilted the screen in Roman's direction, pointing at the gold frame that held a smiling Amelie, standing outside of a bakery with her arms spread wide, looking up at the name: Remy's Sweet Treats.

Roman looked at the photo and then at Wyatt and then back at that photo, his plump lips curling up at the corners. "That has to be what she meant. She hid the page here, with her 'son.' Not only the name, but she's given interviews where she talks about her bakeries as if they were children. It has to be there."

Roman set the phone down, grabbed Wyatt's face in both hands, and pushed in for a kiss. His smile jumped to Wyatt, his freckled cheeks dimpling.

A swell of pride filled him. He was happy, nearly ecstatic, really. It was a welcome change from the helplessness he felt as he hid behind a couch and watched Phantom bleed out. There had been *many* moments these last few days that made him wonder if saying yes to another one of Roman's wild plans was a good idea.

But there were other moments—the quiet ones, the passionate ones—that made him realize regretting anything was just a certified waste of time. Regret did nothing but gnaw away at his insides without giving anything back in return. It was a parasite, taking and taking and taking. Making doubts grow like weeds, working to strangle off any positivity and hope that might exist.

Wyatt was done with that. He was here because he was meant to be. He had nothing to regret, and that extended all the way back to the life-altering decisions he'd made in college, in part led by Roman himself. The past couple of years had been *filled* with regret, weighing him down and suffocating any kind of happiness he tried to hold onto. It left him without energy or inspiration, turning him into a zombie at work and a not-so-much better version of that at home. He lost interest in coding his side projects, and he stopped looking for new opportunities, anything that could get him out of working at the Science Museum.

And it was all because he'd been so focused on

"what if I never listened to Roman, never hacked into the school, never got kicked out and blacklisted."

He had his answer. If he stayed on track, if he lived life according to his preconceived plan, then he wouldn't be riding in the back of a van through the streets of Paris, working with a crew of people who welcomed him in like family from the start. So all that regret he was harboring? It was all for nothing, energy wasted on holding himself back.

No more. He was valuable, he was where he needed to be, and he was going to see this all through. Wyatt was going to change him and his sister's life in a way that wouldn't even be possible in their dreams.

Roman leaned forward, a gentle hand on Phantom's ankle. He was resting his head on a pillow Doc had produced, smiling as she dabbed his forehead with a wet cloth. "How you feeling, Phantom?"

"Like I've been shot in the chest." He gave a grim chuckle and a wink. "Other than that, fine. Bummed that I lost my watch, I guess? Thankfully, that's all I got to worry about. Doc is a miracle worker. I don't know who blessed your hands, but they deserve a Nobel Peace Prize or something."

"I would also like to thank whoever blessed your hands," Bang Bang said from the front seat, finger raised in the air.

Doc arched a plucked brow, her nose ring catching the light of the setting sun. "Watch yourself before these blessed hands go in for a slap."

"Just say the word and I'll drop my pants." Bang Bang looked into the rearview mirror, smirking at a blushing Doc. "Oh, you mean across my face. *Ah, bueno.*"

She rolled her eyes and said something under her breath about him being a silly oaf.

"Mustang, can you get us to the nearest train station?" Roman asked, leaning across Mimic so he could be heard. "We're taking a trip to London tonight. Mimic, will you come with? Doc and Bang Bang, stay behind and watch over Phantom."

Roman turned to Wyatt, light green eyes twinkling like jewels. There was an effortlessness to the way Roman led, something he'd always had even as a kid. People would naturally fall back and hand the reins over to the man with the charismatic eyes and sharp smile. He exuded intelligence and not in a way that made others feel less than, but beyond that, he gave off a sense of confidence that was incomparable to anyone else Wyatt interacted with.

"You can stay behind or come with Mimic and me."

Wyatt didn't take long at all to consider his answer. "I'll go with you guys." He smiled, the thrill of the day washing over him, creating a buzz in the air around him. No regrets, no holding back.

"You sure, Salt?" Roman asked, concern inching into his expression. "You'll be safer here at the hotel. I don't think The Pride knows where the page is, so we might have the advantage here, but still. They've managed to surprise us over and over again."

"I'm sure," Wyatt said. "So long as I'm near you, I feel pretty safe."

The concern evaporated off Roman's face, replaced by a crinkle around the corners of his eyes that gave away just how happy he was.

No regrets, ever.

Chapter 21

Roman Ashford

The train made its way through the French countryside, the windows framing a sight that was made for film. The rolling green hills and expansive vineyards, mixing with tiny French towns and farms, were romantic, dreamy, and Roman couldn't really appreciate any of it. His thoughts were consumed with the heist, with what went wrong and what he could have done to prevent it. He was the leader of this crew, and he'd failed them today, failed Phantom. Thankfully he was going to be fine, thanks to Doc's skill and quick thinking, but things easily could have taken a turn.

He leaned back in his seat, stretching his legs. Mimic was on another aisle, reading one of her favorite books and sipping on some coffee. Wyatt was walking back down to the seat, tucking his phone

The Sunset Job

back into his pocket. He squeezed past Roman's knees and sat down, smiling.

"How is she?" Roman asked.

"Good, good. She's back at home now. She said the guy you sent to protect her is actually really hot. I think there might be a thing between them."

Roman gave a chuckle. "Freddy's been a good friend for years now, and he's a good guy. Julie would be a great match for him."

"Well, she wanted me to pass on her thanks for letting her live out her best *Bodyguard* fantasy."

"Anytime," Roman said, giving Wyatt a wink. Having the freckle-faced guy sitting next to him was an instant balm to all of Roman's persistent worries and questions. "Remember in high school when you had me pretend I was your bodyguard walking through the mall?"

Wyatt cocked his head, thought on it, then started to laugh. "Yup, I remember. Hm, guess bodyguard fantasies run in the family."

"Guess so."

"To be fair, I was being bullied pretty bad, and having you walking next to me in an oversized suit from Walmart and some cheap glasses really did the trick."

Roman nodded, remembering some of the taunts they'd hurl at Wyatt. He was an easy target for them. Skinny, quiet, slightly awkward, swimming in great grades, and seemingly allergic to any sports.

Plus, him being openly gay didn't help much. Not back then, when kids actively sought the biggest, brightest, most colorful targets to hit. Roman had found Wyatt to be one of the bravest people he'd ever met, and he inspired Roman to come out himself. At the time, Roman was a quarterback of a (very modestly) successful high school team and had a line of cheerleaders trying to get with him. When news spread that he was out and proud, the school was rocked.

More so when he showed up to first period holding the hand of a boy who'd had him fixated from the very first day he laid eyes on him.

"Now I'm the one rescuing you," Wyatt teased, turning his honey-brown gaze out the window. The train entered a tunnel and created a mosaic of dark stone blurring past.

"You are," Roman said. He wasn't even joking about that. His sincerity carried on his tone, causing Wyatt to look over, curious. "There's something you don't know about, Salt. Something that happened to me in the time you were gone."

Wyatt sat up, his thin brows furrowing. "What happened?"

Roman rubbed his forehead. This was heavy, much more so than anything he'd opened up about in the past. But he had to get it off his chest, lifted from his heart. He needed to tell Wyatt what happened.

"My uncle wasn't the only important person I've

lost. There was someone, a man. Harry 'Torpedo' Montenegro. We met working one of my uncle's jobs and became inseparable. I started feeling things with him that I'd only ever felt once before, and that scared me. It really fucked scared me, because I also knew how much it hurt when things didn't work out. Like a fucking stab directly through the rib cage, over and over again.

"But I let myself fall. Harry and I got together three months after my uncle passed and were together for two years. We were working a job in Brazil, having the time of our lives, when I decided to act on some bad intel. Walked us directly into a trap set up, and only one of us made it out alive."

Wyatt blinked away some of the shock. Roman didn't want to hurt Wyatt by telling him this, about him being with another man, but he couldn't stay silent about it, either. It was a part of his history, molding his current actions; it was only fair for Wyatt to see the full picture.

"Damn, I'm sorry," Wyatt said, his hands forming an anxious bundle in his lap. Was he upset? "Really, I am."

"I don't want to hurt you by telling you this, you know that, right?"

"I'm not hurt." Wyatt shook his head, eyes locked with Roman's. The train rode out of the tunnel, and the car filled with a warm glow from the setting sun, its rays slashing over the peaks of a verdant green hillside. "I'm completely aware of the fact that our lives kept going even after we weren't together. I'm happy you told me, actually. I want to know, about everything. I feel like there are so many blank pages between us that need to be filled."

Roman grinned, unable to stop himself from wrapping an arm around Wyatt's shoulders. "Let's fill them, then. What's the funniest thing that's happened to you since we've been apart?"

"The funniest thing... hmm. I guess when me and Julie were at the grocery store and someone thought I was Andrew Garfield. She started to relentlessly hit on me until she saw Julie and thought she was my girlfriend, to which Julie replied, 'Absolutely the fuck not. He's my brother, gay, and is more like Andrew Gar-meadow than Andrew Garfield.' Yeah, I'd say that's been one of the funniest things."

Roman gave a hearty laugh at that. "I do see the resemblance, though."

"Yeah, whatever. How about you? What's the funniest thing that's happened?"

Roman clicked his tongue and tossed around a couple of memories, landing on one of the most vivid ones. "Probably when Bang Bang and I were in Santorini, on a break between jobs. We were partying on a yacht when Bang Bang tells me he was disappearing to go hook up with someone he's had his eyes on, so I give him the good-luck slap on the ass and send him on his merry way. Ten minutes later

The Sunset Job

and I hear a commotion. Turns out someone brought a goat onto the yacht, and it ended up bursting into the room, causing him to run out naked and scared. I locked the goat in a bathroom, and we became best friends ever since."

Wyatt laughed, shaking his head. "It's wild to me how my story started in a Piggly Wiggly store, and yours started in a dreamy vacation spot while floating around on a yacht with a wild goat. God, our lives are so different."

"Not anymore, Salt."

"No... I guess not, huh?" Wyatt turned to look out the window.

"Do you regret coming along? Saying yes when I asked for your help?"

He sucked on his bottom lip, and Roman had the sudden and icy-cold fear that he'd say yes. That Wyatt would admit to thinking this was all a huge mistake and that he wanted off the crazy ride the second the opportunity presented itself. Roman would never let go of the guilt.

"I don't. Maybe at first, but I've realized that everything is happening like it's supposed to. I'm a big control freak, you know that, but I've been able to let some of that go. And I've let my regrets go, too."

Roman swallowed. His next question was heavy but sincere. "Did you ever think of me as a regret?"

Wyatt sucked in a breath. He licked his lips, looked out the window, shook his head. Roman watched every single twitch, every minute shift in body posture. His heart raced as if he were in the middle of a gunfight.

"If I'm completely honest... yes. There was a point in my life that I wished we had never met. But, also being completely honest here, that didn't last very long. Even when I was sulking in my own depression, going to the same shitty jobs day in and day out, just trying to keep mine and my sister's heads above water, even then I didn't regret you. All I really did was regret not looking for you."

The words rang true, and Roman felt the brakes kick on somewhere around his left and right ventricles, his pulse slowing back to a regular rate. "You were always great about letting go of grudges."

"I just hate drama. Why hold on to all the negative when you can just focus on the positive? Like being here with you, on a train to freaking London. My high school sweetheart turned college enemy turned adult... something."

"Adult *boyfriend*?"

Wyatt cocked his head, eyes narrowing and smile growing. "Yeah, yeah, I think that works."

There, as simple—and as complicated—as that, they were together. Officially. Like back when they were starry-eyed kids walking through their high school halls. Their lives took many twists and turns to get there, but there they were. Roman reached for Wyatt's hand, twining their fingers together. The conductor came on through the speakers and announced they were only a half hour away from the St. Pancras Station, their stop in London.

They spent the rest of the train ride reminiscing about their first few dates and talking about recreating them, glowing in their new-boyfriend status, both of them laughing at anything and smiling as if they'd each won the lotto. Roman soaked it in, bathing in the warm happiness that surrounded them. He understood exactly how powerful these moments were and how fleeting they could sometimes be. How life enjoyed playing tricks, taking as much as it gave, pulling out the rug to reveal the floor underneath was a trap door full of lava.

The train dinged and slowed to a stop, just as Wyatt and Roman were recalling a scandalous encounter they'd had in a hotel hot tub. Mimic stood and walked over to them, a book tucked under her arm and a knowing smile playing on her face.

"You guys had a good ride?"

"Very," Roman said. "Now, let's go steal ourselves that page."

Chapter 22

Wyatt Hernandez

Boyfriends.

Again.

Wyatt had to admit he was surprised, probably the most surprised he'd been by anything on this job yet. He didn't think that title would be coming, even though their physical chemistry clearly hadn't gone anywhere. If anything, it had actually grown more intense. The passage of time and the physical space that separated them made it all the more sweeter when that space was annihilated, when their bodies were united all over again.

It was a second chance; not many relationships were given those. He never imagined his being one of them, but he was so very glad it was.

The trio walked down a narrow street lined with townhomes, turning a corner and finding themselves next to a local deli with its storefront painted a deep

The Sunset Job

blue, a row of restaurants and pubs following it, broken apart by a bright green cross advertising a pharmacy (and not a dispensary like Wyatt initially thought). Mimic led the pack, her slicked-backed hair falling in a sheet of inky black down to her shoulders, a trendy pair of sunglasses covering her eagle-like eyes. The bright red of her lip popped against the dark black of her jacket and pants, a huge contrast to the turquoise-worshipping wedding planner she'd been portraying just hours earlier.

"How do you like London so far?" Mimic asked over her shoulder.

"I'm legit thinking I could move here. And I've barely even seen any of it."

Roman chuckled, reaching for Wyatt's hand and taking it in his. "Maybe we can plan a leisure trip when all this is over. I want to show you around. London is one of my favorite cities, but so are the ones around it. Oxford is like a classic fairy-tale book, and the Cotswolds is dreamy, too. It's basically a bunch of villages that stood the test of time."

"There's no comparison between this and my neighborhood back in Miami. Although I think I would miss my weekly dose of Publix subs if I moved out here."

Roman squeezed his hand. "I'm sure you can find a suitable replacement."

A red double-decker bus drove past them as they waited to cross the street, the bakery directly ahead of them. People were sat outside, eating their pastries and sipping their coffees, none of them aware of what had gone down hours earlier with the owner of their favorite bakery. Wyatt felt a pang of sadness reverberate through him. It wasn't his fault or his doing that caused Amelie to lose her life, but he still couldn't help but feel a thread of responsibility tying him to the death.

And now here they were, ready to walk into her bakery and steal something left behind by her son. Wyatt would need to be on his best behavior after this to make sure his karma leveled out.

"Alright," Roman said, stopping them next to an entrance to the underground. A flurry of businesspeople filtered out with their suits and their briefcases, some of them heading toward the bakery for an after-work snack. "We have no idea where she's hidden the page, so this makes things a little complicated. Mimic, were you able to get the paperwork and badges on the train ride over?"

She nodded and pulled a neatly folded paper out of her clutch. Opening it, she revealed it to be an inspection notice, along with matching name badges. Wyatt blinked in shocked surprise, once again astounded at Mimic's ability to pull together believable covers for them.

"Perfect," Roman said, grabbing it. "Wyatt and I will go in as inspectors, and we'll search every single corner of the bakery while you go in as a high-profile

The Sunset Job

and *extremely* demanding customer. Distract the employees while we snoop around."

Mimic nodded, dropping her glasses to reveal a wink. "Bitch mode activated." She turned and strutted down the street, lithe legs walking as gracefully as if she were putting on a ballet. A couple of men (and multiple women) tried to be subtle in checking her out but were given away by their slack jaws and drool trail they left in their wake.

"Ready, Salt?"

"Let's do this." Wyatt looked down at Roman's name badge. "Lester."

"Seriously, Mimic couldn't pick a less attractive name for me."

"Mine's Giovanni. I don't mind that."

"Gio suits you. Lester, though? I feel like I should be cast in the next Addam's Family reboot."

"You could be the walking hand since you're so good at using yours." Wyatt shot him a wink. Flirting didn't always come naturally to him, but he guessed that changed when the flirting was aimed at his boyfriend.

Roman chuckled, smiling wide as they crossed the street. "Or maybe a walking penis, since you seemed to enjoy that about me, too. Judging by how you were shouting, 'Yes, Roman, please, *please* give me that big juicy co—'"

"Okay, I got the point. You have options." Wyatt's cheeks flushed pink, matching the rush of warmth that spread down his back and settled somewhere around his crotch. He tried to ignore the tightening feeling that worked its way into his core, focusing instead on the job at hand.

They entered the bakery, finding it very similar to the one located in Paris. The walls were smooth oak with expensive detailing, each of the displays well-lit and magically arranged, highlighting all kinds of tasty desserts and pastries. There was a photo wall in this bakery as well, but unlike the last one, every photo on this wall featured Amelie's son, from the day he was born to the day he stood next to his mom at the opening of her Paris location. It was clear this bakery was made with the love of her son at the forefront.

Unfortunately, it was her son who kicked off the chain of events that would take both their lives.

"No, no, you don't understand. I need this order filled by *tonight*. I have a dinner set with three Oscar-winning directors and ten of my good friends—you might have seen them walking Rihanna's Fenty show." Mimic had three employees cornered, all of them looking at each other with doe-like eyes, wondering who the hell was going to rescue them from this demanding and slightly unhinged customer.

Roman caught the attention of the least flustered employee. She pushed a curly strand of red hair off her slightly sweaty forehead and walked around the

The Sunset Job

counter, apparently relieved she was thrown a life raft out of that conversation. "Hi, how can I help you two today?"

Roman tapped the name badge on his chest. "We're here for an inspection. Shouldn't take very long. We'll just need to get any of the keys for the back rooms and such."

Did Roman just throw on a British accent, or was that Wyatt's imagination? Mimic definitely spoke with one, but Roman wasn't as well versed in disguises as she was.

"Oh... we just had the inspectors here last week."

Shit. They hadn't accounted for that. And still, without missing a beat, Roman continued on. "We know, we got their report. There's just a couple things we have to look over. That's all."

He flashed her that disarming grin of his, those starry green eyes crinkling at the corners, inviting her to say anything but no.

"Right, of course. Here." She pulled out a set of jingling keys from a pocket in her apron. "Just bring them back to me. I'm the manager." She shot an apprehensive look toward Mimic and the two other boys, who were slowly inching away from the increasingly angry famous woman who they'd never seen in their entire lives. "I should go handle that. Let me know if you two need anything else."

She went back behind the counter, confronting Mimic in the way a lion tamer would—chest out and mannerisms set to larger than life in hopes of distracting some of her fury.

"I'll start out here," Roman said. They were both wearing blue T-shirts and khaki shorts, although the shirts were a different shade, and the shorts were different lengths (Roman's being short enough to hug his muscular upper thigh). They still looked the part. All Wyatt had to do was rummage around and find the page; it shouldn't be too difficult. Especially considering no one had started shooting yet.

"I'll take the back rooms," Wyatt said. He left Roman in the front of the store, searching underneath baguette baskets and behind some of the framed photos. The employees were far too busy putting out Mimic's fire to notice Roman's odd way of inspecting a bakery. Meanwhile, Wyatt disappeared through a set of double doors, walking into a hallway washed in fluorescent light, the white brick walls bare of any art or photos, instead displaying various workplace rules and policies. Wyatt took a right and entered the kitchens, greeted by three bakers, all working on separate stations.

He couldn't imagine Amelie choosing the kitchen as a good hiding place, but he certainly wasn't going to overlook it, either. He started to open the drawers and cabinets, finding nothing but baking dishes and supplies.

By the time he got to the refrigerator, he could already tell the bakers' eyes were pinned to his back.

The Sunset Job

They'd seen actual inspectors come in and out of the bakery, and Wyatt doubted any of them acted the way he was acting.

He turned and looked at the bakers, none of them looking very happy at the intrusion. "Looks like, uh, it all checks out. Thank you—blokes."

Blokes? What in the "tea and crumpets" hell got into me?

He turned away from the confused bakers before any of them could spot the blush of embarrassment coloring his cheeks. This was why he enjoyed working with computers instead of people. Anything dumb he might write down in a code could easily be deleted and rewritten—not exactly so with actual conversations.

He scurried out of the kitchens and back into the hall. There were only a couple of doors left. Wyatt checked one and found a pristine bathroom, the scent of pine-scented floor cleaner drifting out after he closed the door. The next door was locked, so he grabbed the ring of keys and tried out a couple, not taking long to find the one that fit.

Behind the locked door was Amelie's office.

This had to be where the page was hidden. Had to be. Wyatt looked over his shoulder and made sure there weren't any prying eyes as he entered the office, closing the door behind him as quietly as he could manage. The paranoia was beginning to enter from stage left, no doubt affected by the fact that the last two parts of this job involved a lot of guns and blood. It seemed like they were ahead of the Pride on this one, but he couldn't be completely sure of that. The only guarantee of getting out safely was moving quickly. The faster he got hold of the page, the sooner they could get back on a plane and be that much closer to the finish line.

Thankfully, Amelie hadn't splurged much on her office. It was a small space with minimal decorations and furniture. Only a desk and a computer, with a tall and banged-up filing cabinet sitting next to it. Wyatt started there, going through every drawer and finding nothing but recipes and business documents.

The bottommost drawer had a lock, giving Wyatt the most hope of finding what he needed inside. He went through the ring of keys, fumbling through them until he reached the last one. The key slipped into the lock and turned, and he held his breath as he opened it.

Had to be, it had to be in the—

Nothing. Nothing but some sensitive tax documents and a couple of other emails, appearing to be way too private for Wyatt to rummage through.

Damn it. Nothing.

He did a slow circle, not spotting many more hiding places. He looked at the computer, a picture of her son smiling from the corner of the blank screen. Wyatt cocked his head. Could she have...

He pulled out the chair and rolled his neck, loud

pops filling the tiny room. He tapped the keyboard, and the screen lit up, showing a smiling Amelie with an arm over her son, a password prompt underneath.

Simple stuff.

It took Wyatt a total of five minutes to boot the computer back up in administrator mode and finagle through the different screens, going past the log-in screen and directly to the desktop. It was a cluttered mess of useless screenshots and programs that hadn't seen the light of day since they were installed. He sorted through them, looking for anything that seemed off or different. If she was hiding the page on her computer, it would likely be inside of a folder inside of another folder inside of one more.

He did a preliminary search, looking for obviously dumb keywords and finding none of them. A sound on the other side of the door made him freeze, nearly unplugging the computer from the wall in a blind panic. A health and safety inspector would have a lot of explaining to do if they were caught looking through the dead owner's computer.

Whoever made the sound disappeared down the hall. Wyatt breathed out a sigh of relief and got back to work. This was his territory; it was his gig. He considered himself a cyber bloodhound, and now was his chance to prove his skills.

He clicked through on a folder titled "For Tomorrow" and was instantly greeted with another password prompt.

Interesting development. Sounds a lot like the Tome of Tomorrow.

This one was a little harder to crack. Whatever program she used to secure her folders was pretty advanced but not advanced enough to evade Wyatt's digital detective skills. He cracked through and found himself on the other side without even breaking a sweat.

"Yes!" he said, catching himself and keeping his voice low, even though his excitement was off the charts.

He'd done it. On the screen, stretching from edge to edge, was a single scanned document. The page they were after. Right there, in front of him. And he'd been the one to find it.

He downloaded the scan and sent it to himself. With the page in hand, he shut the computer down and slipped back out of the office, a grin stretching from ear to ear. He walked back out into the front of the bakery, where Roman was inspecting the underside of a macaron tray while Mimic shouted about how many social media followers she had.

Roman looked at Wyatt and spotted the grin, getting up off his knees and going over to meet him. All Wyatt had to say was "Got it," and Roman nearly did the Flintstones leap. Mimic must have heard as she wrapped up her conversation with "You know what, it's fine. I don't like sweets anyway," before

The Sunset Job

turning around and leaving the befuddled employees watching the three disappear out of the bakery.

"What in the world was that about?" the manager asked.

One of the employees shrugged and said, "I don't know. These days you get a thousand followers and a few candle sponsorships and you think you're a celebrity. Ridiculous."

Chapter 23

Wyatt Hernandez

THE MOOD on the plane was celebratory, champagne bottles being popped and loud music being played. Even Phantom, who was lying back in a seat with his legs up on another, was raising a glass to Wyatt's success. They may have been a mile high into the sky, but Wyatt felt like they were flying much higher than that.

He'd done it. He proved his worth, carried his weight. There was no longer any doubt that he deserved the prize at the end of this job, if there ever was any to begin with.

He drank the last bit of champagne in his glass before Bang Bang poured him another, telling him to open his mouth and pouring some directly down his throat. It fizzed around his lips, bubbles popping on his tongue. He wiped his mouth with the back of a hand, Bang Bang taking him into a side hug and chugging some of the champagne himself before setting the bottle down and letting out a plane-shaking burp.

"Bang Bang!" Doc said from her seat, eyes wide.

Wyatt laughed, stumbling a little as he sat down in the chair next to her. Bang Bang blew her a kiss before going to play cards with Mustang, Mimic, and Roman.

"We should call him Burp Burp instead," Doc said with a roll of her eyes and a growing smile on her lips. She set down the historical romance she was reading, the cover catching Wyatt's eyes.

"You were incredible, by the way." Tipsy Wyatt tended to spill over with compliments and fawning. "The way you handled things in the van. I've never seen anything like that, and I've watched all thirteen seasons of *Grey's Anatomy*."

That got a laugh out of Doc. She fiddled with the pink band that wrapped up her tight ponytail. "Thank you. It's what I love to do—heal people. Ever since I was little. I was the house nurse."

"Is that where you started learning?"

She nodded, looking out the small window at a clear blue sky, stretching for what appeared to be infinity. "It is, actually. My dad's a cardiovascular surgeon, one of the best in the country. Came from Korea with his parents when he was only four, and he was similar to me—obsessed with medicine even at that age. He taught me a lot, but not all. I learned so much from spending a couple years with Tibetan Buddhists, absorbing every little thing I could from them." She gave Wyatt a wink. "And then, of course, there's *Grey's Anatomy*."

"So what brings you to the Rainbow's Seven? Why not go the traditional route, follow in your dad's footsteps."

Doc nodded, turning her gaze back out the window. "That's a really good question with a very complicated answer. Short version: I became disillusioned with the medical field and wanted to make a difference some other way. Plus, I made some really bad bets that I've now got to pay off, and a surgeon's salary wouldn't even cut it."

Wyatt's eyebrows rose, the champagne flooding his system making it difficult to control his expressions. Doc didn't strike him as the gambling type, but it must have been a pretty big hole she dug herself if it couldn't be paid off without completing this job.

"What's the long version? If you don't mind me asking." Wyatt hated to pry, but on the flip side of that token, he also wanted to get to know Doc some more. Each member of the Rainbow's Seven had surprised him one way or another, all of them feeling like family more and more with every passing day. It wasn't something Wyatt ever expected to feel when he signed up for this, but he wasn't opposed to it, either.

"I don't mind," Doc said, reaching for her bag of

sour worms and popping a few of the colorful candies into her mouth. But before she could continue, their conversation was cut short by a new addition: Monica "Mustang" Mercedes, smiling as she chugged down some beer.

"You seem happy," Doc said.

"I won two hundred bucks just now. I'm *very* happy." She put a hand behind her head and relaxed into the chair. "What are you guys talking about? Seems really sad over here."

Doc and Wyatt both laughed, not minding the interruption, although Wyatt did want to hear that long version at some point. "We were just talking about our reasons for being here," Doc said.

Monica nodded, licking her lips before taking another sip. Suddenly, it was like those two hundred dollars disappeared, along with the grin on her face.

"What's yours?" Wyatt asked, apparently as forward as he was complimentary after he'd had a few drinks.

"Revenge," Monica said, point-blank.

"Oh..." Wyatt wasn't expecting that answer. Not with the amount of money on the line. He assumed everyone here was driven by how fat their bank accounts would get after it was all said and done. With money came power, came the power to *change*. They'd all have enough money to make a difference, not only in their own lives but in their loved ones' lives.

"For what?" he asked.

Doc fiddled with her ponytail again, keeping her eyes down at the floor. Mustang took another chug. "For love—what else is revenge for? I used to love someone, someone I shouldn't have but that I couldn't help. It came on fast and fierce. Burned brighter than anything I'd felt up to that point in my life.

"Her name was Vero. She was everything to me. She was also Leonidas' wife."

That pulled a shocked gasp from Wyatt, again the drinks having lowered his ability to control his face.

"Right, well, Leonidas found out. And he had her killed. The sick fucking bastard had her tortured and killed. He sent me the video and then sent me a finger of hers a day. It was horrific, and it changed me. It really fucking changed me."

Wyatt became nauseous. He normally did fine on planes, but this conversation would have made his stomach flip even if they were on solid ground. He considered reaching for a bag just in case all that champagne decided to fight back.

"Jesus, I'm so sorry," Wyatt said, absolutely positive the words did nothing to heal her pain, but at least they were *something*.

"It's okay. I'll make things even for my Vero. She deserves at least that."

The Sunset Job

That had taken a turn. Wyatt wasn't sure how to steer the conversation back to less rocky terrain.

"What was she like?" he asked, deciding to focus on the positives.

"One of the funniest people I knew," Mustang said, the dark shadow across her face lifting, brightened by her honey-brown eyes, a small birthmark next to her eyebrow popping off her tan skin. "She had a comeback for *anything*. And she loved cars, too. Loved to come to my races, cheer me on. She was such a positive presence in my life, it was—it was difficult when she was gone." Mustang sucked in a deep breath, looking over her shoulder, fondness in her gaze as her eyes landed on a napping Mimic. "I was saved, though. A month after Vero's death, when I thought I was going to just drive off a bridge and end it all, that's when I met Roman and Mimic. It was at a dive bar. They were there drinking after finishing a job, and I was there drinking to become as numb as possible. When I found out they were working against the Pride, well, it was like a sign from up above. I joined up with Roman and didn't look back. Falling in love with Mimic was a nice bonus." Mustang wore a genuine smile, one that must have taken so much strength to pull off. After witnessing the horrors she had, Wyatt wouldn't have blamed her if she never smiled again.

"You and Mimic make such a great couple," Doc

said. "It's like you were each made for each other. It's obvious when you two look at each other."

Wyatt nodded, agreeing with Doc's assessment. "There's a lot of intermingling in this crew, huh?"

"It's like showing up to the bar after a softball game," Mustang said. "Everyone's either seen, licked, touched, or fucked someone else in that bar. The Queer Degrees of Separation, I like to call it. As long as things don't get complicated between anyone, then we're good."

Doc sucked her tongue. She reached down and grabbed her book. "But don't things always manage to get complicated, somehow or another?"

"Maybe in the books you read, but sometimes I like to think life can smooth itself out. If I'm scared of turning every corner or constantly worried about when something gets fucked up, then I'd be missing out on so much." Mustang grabbed her beer and raised it in an invisible cheer. "To winning two hundred dollars and getting laid later."

Wyatt lifted his glass with a laugh and clinked it against Mustang's. Doc smirked but lifted her book and kept her face buried inside it.

That appeared to be Mustang's cue to stand and walk over to a sleeping Mimic, stepping over her with care and sitting down in the chair next to her, maneuvering Mimic so that she could rest her head on Mustang's shoulder.

Wyatt scanned the plane, spotting Roman

The Sunset Job

toward the back having a conversation with Bang Bang and Phantom. It didn't seem to be an important one, judging by Bang Bang's boisterous laughter, so Wyatt decided to interrupt them. He stood, but instead of walking toward them, he turned and headed toward the front of the plane.

He brought out his phone and sent Roman a text with a single word:

Bathroom?

Chapter 24

Roman Ashford

THE FLIGHT back home felt like a victory lap for Roman. He was well aware that they still had one more hurdle to jump before they crossed the finish line, but that didn't dim anyone's celebratory light. The crew was flying as high as the plane was, and Roman couldn't have been prouder. They certainly earned the five bottles of champagne that were all mostly empty already.

"Maybe my next tattoo will be one of your face, *broki*. If you get us as much money as you say you will, then I think you'd deserve it."

Roman scoffed. "Where would you get it, on your other arm?"

Bang Bang, wearing a white tank top, turned to show off the colorful tattoo that took up most of his right bicep. The gay pin-up guy seemed to be winking at Roman.

The Sunset Job

"I think I'll put you on a leg instead. I don't want anything competing with Tito." He patted his arm lovingly and gave the tattoo a kiss.

"Which leg?" Roman asked.

"My third leg, obviously."

Roman rolled his eyes and laughed along with Bang Bang. "You'll need to pick a tattoo artist that knows how to work with small designs, then."

Bang Bang's eyebrows jolted upward at the unexpected read.

Roman's phone buzzed, pulling his attention downward. Bang Bang said something that must have been a comeback, but Roman quit paying attention to him the second he read the text.

"Bathroom?" Wyatt asked.

Roman looked up, spotting Wyatt as he slipped into the bathroom, closing the door behind him. He cut Bang Bang off, standing. "Sorry, bathroom break."

Bang Bang must not have noticed Wyatt entering the bathroom first, or he would have said something. Instead, he put a hand on his forehead and gave a salute, sitting back in his seat and opening his phone, likely to look up the score on whatever football game was happening or which drag queen won yesterday's episode on one of his favorite TV shows. Bang Bang was a man of many interests, and so was Roman.

Except he only had one interest in this moment.

He opened the bathroom door and went inside,

nearly tripping over Wyatt in the cramped space. It didn't take longer than a second for their lips to collide, their bodies pushing together, both of them already hard. Roman swallowed a moan from Wyatt's throat as his hand went around and grabbed on Wyatt's ass, pulling him closer, tongues lashing together. The taste of the kiss was more intoxicating than any amount of champagne could be.

"Think anyone saw?" Wyatt asked as he worked to pull off Roman's pants.

"I don't give a flying fuck."

"Fair enough."

Wyatt licked his lips as he dropped Roman's jeans to his ankles, revealing a white-and-pink jockstrap underneath, his hard cock already slipping out through the side.

"You hated wearing these when we were younger," Wyatt noted, running his hand across Roman's length.

"I didn't have good taste back then."

"Clearly." Wyatt took his shorts and briefs off, his dick springing free with a bounce that hypnotized Roman. "Speaking of taste," Wyatt said with a smirk as he lowered himself to his knees. He leaned in and sucked the precome off the tip, swirling his tongue around the head and taking more of Roman into his mouth. The plane rocked on a stretch of rough air, causing Roman to reach out and grab the sink for some stability.

The Sunset Job

Wyatt gagged, taking more of Roman than he was ready for. He pulled back, a string of saliva connecting him to Roman's cock. He licked it up with a smile, looking up with tears dabbing at the corners of his eyes. "Got to be careful with the turbulence."

He went back in, slurping and sucking and stroking. Roman's entire body, from toes to scalp, tingled with a euphoric buzz, allowing him to relax every single muscle, his hands encasing Wyatt's head and gently rubbing as Wyatt worshiped his cock.

"That's it," Roman growled, his head falling back. "Look up at me, Salt. Look into my eyes while you swallow me whole."

Wyatt listened, his big amber eyes locking with Roman, the freckles on his face seeming to dance as Roman's cock pushed against his cheeks.

"Fuck, Salt, you already have me close." Roman put a thumb against Wyatt's lips, hooking it in and stretching, watching Wyatt's mouth open and his cock plunging inside. He couldn't believe there was a time when he didn't have this, when he'd lost the chance to be with the man of his wildest and steamiest dreams. No other man brought him as much pleasure sucking him off, not the way Wyatt did. He always took his time, always looked like he wanted Roman's nut more than anything else in the world. A reverence in the way his lips softly kissed up and down his shaft before wrapping around him and taking him back down his throat.

He was going to come, he was so fucking close. The animalistic grunts escaping him were a dead giveaway, which frustrated him immensely when Wyatt stopped. He looked up with his lips shining and his eyes glowing, the slant in his smile turning devilish.

"Turn around," Wyatt said. He had a hand between his own legs and was stroking his thick cock, a trimmed bush of dark hair crowning it. Roman nearly told him to stand, wanting that hard length rubbing against his, but Wyatt spoke again, a hungry command tinting his words. "Turn. Around."

Roman listened. He braced himself on the wall and pushed his ass back, Wyatt moaning as he grabbed both cheeks in his hands. Roman didn't always like his ass getting played with, but Wyatt changed all of that. He found that it was really all about the comfort he had in Wyatt, allowing him to experience all new heights of bliss.

Roman relaxed further, jerking himself off as Wyatt spread his ass and spit, the sound hitting him before the warmth did. Roman twitched forward before taking a breath and letting go, Wyatt's thumb exploring between his wet crack, rubbing over his hole, sending another spasm out from his balls.

"Mhmm," Wyatt said, fingers exploring, soft

The Sunset Job

kisses landing on either cheek. He opened Roman again and asked, "Can I?"

Roman knew exactly what he meant, his "Yes" coming out strangled with a moan. Wyatt pushed forward, burying his face in Roman's ass, his tongue flicking up and down, his entire face moving with it. The scratchiness of his shaved face added another layer of sensation that Roman wasn't prepared for. His vision tunneled, balls tightening. He bit down on a knuckle to stop himself from crying out.

He ground his ass back, practically sitting on Wyatt's face, the orgasm racing toward him with the speed of a bullet train.

"I'm gonna come," Roman said, grabbing his cock just as it exploded, Wyatt continuing to tongue his ass. He moaned into Roman, his own orgasm crashing through, ropes of come from the both of them mixing together on the floor.

Chuckles escaped them as Wyatt got back up onto his feet, helped by a spent Roman, their dicks beginning to soften, wet and still-dripping tips rubbing together.

"Gah damn," Roman said, kissing Wyatt, tasting the sex still on his lips. "I think I almost passed out."

"That good, huh?"

"Very," Roman said, wrapping his arms around Wyatt, his heart feeling just as warm and sparkly as the rest of him. It was an effervescent kind of sensation, like he was seconds away from floating up and joining the rest of the clouds they were flying through.

"Today was a good day." Wyatt melted into Roman's body, resting his head against Roman's chest. "Not only did I get to join the mile-high club, but we also grabbed the page. Without any Pride interference."

"You're right," Roman said, nodding and gently kissing Wyatt's forehead. He could stay locked in this embrace for all of eternity, and he would be the happiest fucking man alive. "I'm trying to think of what differentiated this time from the last."

"Everyone was in that van when we spoke about the bakery, so if there was a traitor..."

He reached around Wyatt and turned the sink on. Just in case. "Not everyone could hear us, though."

Wyatt cocked his head. "Huh?"

"Mustang and Bang Bang, sitting up front, they had a difficult time hearing. Bang Bang even asked me earlier what it was we were saying back there."

The shocked disbelief slipped into Wyatt's tone as he whispered his next questions. "Do you think it's Mustang? Bang Bang?"

Roman shook his head, even the suggestion weighing heavy on his heart. "I don't know what to think right now," he whispered under the sound of running water. "I can't imagine a world where either of them would betray us, and that's what scares me the most. It makes me feel like there's a blind spot I'm missing. I just don't know what that is."

"With how badly Mustang wants revenge, I don't think she'd be bringing information to the Pride."

Roman shook his head. "No, I don't think so either. But maybe there's something else at play? Maybe by betraying us, she gets closer to Leonidas? Close enough to stab him in the chest."

"And Bang Bang? What would he be motivated by?"

"I have no idea," Roman said, his fingers tracing lazy circles around Wyatt's lower back. "He isn't motivated by money, so they can't buy him out. And he's head over heels for Doc. I can't think of why he'd do anything to hurt her."

"I agree, I don't think it's him, either."

"And that leaves us back at square one. No answers, only questions."

Wyatt picked his head up, resting his chin on Roman's chest, gazes meeting. "Can I get one of my questions answered?"

"Of course, what is it?"

Wyatt sucked his bottom lip, the puffy pink flesh coming back pale from between his teeth. "What are the pages for? What the hell is all of this for? I know there's money involved, but how is this *Tome of Tomorrow* going to be *that* valuable? It was at the Miami Science Museum, not behind some bullet-proof glass at the Louvre."

Roman expected this line of questioning to arise at some point. He'd kept things slightly vague with the crew, for the exact reason that brought up the previous discussion. His uncle had taught him many things, but one of the most vital lessons dealt with trust. He'd always told Roman it was important to trust rarely but powerfully, and to trust in levels. Know that there were layers to a relationship, and not everyone had to know everything all at once. Information could, and should, only be shared on a need-to-know basis.

Roman knew that. He couldn't lead a successful heist without trusting his crew, but he also didn't have to lay out all the cards, either.

Except for Wyatt. It was time he saw the hand Roman was playing with.

"The *Tome of Tomorrow* is a key," Roman started. The plane flew through another bout of light turbulence, rocking them around in the cramped space. "Remy was a savant, and he funneled a lot of his intelligence into making money, aside from making some accurate predictions about the future. He did that through cryptocurrencies, amassing a fortune that rivaled the GDP of a few small countries. When he found out he was dying, he knew he wanted to leave behind a way for someone worthy enough to put the pieces together and collect the money for themselves."

"Crypto?" Wyatt asked with an arched brow.

The Sunset Job

"We could be doing all of this to end up finding the money on the day of a massive crash and end up holding a bag full of pennies?"

Roman chuckled, having foreseen that fear already.

As had Remy.

"We're dealing with a savant who could weirdly seem to predict the future. When he crossed over the two billion mark, Remy cashed in. Turned it all into untraceable, hard and solid cash, digitizing it into his own currency and staked against the US dollar, making it impossible to fluctuate. Inside of the tome, on the first and the last pages, Remy placed the beginning and end of the seed key for the digital wallet that contains the money. The rest of the seed key could be found within the tome, using a legend on the first page.

"He said having the entire seed key wouldn't be enough, though. That there was a puzzle to be solved, a difficult one, one that required hacking through whatever firewalls he placed around the digital wallet."

"And that's where I come in."

Roman nodded. "You'd be the person bringing the torch over the finish line."

"What if I can't get in?" Wyatt's eyes widened, but Roman answered him with a soft kiss, arms still wrapped around him.

"You can. I know you can."

Wyatt smiled, kissing Roman back. "Thank you for telling me. I was beginning to think you were dragging us along on some pyramid scheme."

"Yeah, right. Next, I was going to ask you to start selling moldy leggings."

Wyatt laughed, reaching for some tissue paper. "Alright, let's clean up in here and get back outside before Bang Bang says something stupid."

"Oh, he's for sure going to say something stupid." Roman helped Wyatt clean up their mess before they tugged on their pants, fixing their messed up heads of hair and opening the bathroom door, stepping out at the same time.

"There they are!" Bang Bang said, lifting his bottle of beer. "Can I be the godfather to whatever baby you two made in there?"

"Bruno, stop it." Doc gave Bang Bang a playful slap on the chest but couldn't hide the smile on her face.

Wyatt went to his seat with a blush on his cheeks, smiling as Phantom ribbed him. Roman walked to the back of the plane, every step feeling as if it were on a cloud. Bang Bang continued to tease him for the rest of the trip, but Roman didn't mind. He was flying far too high to be bothered by anything.

Chapter 25

Wyatt Hernandez

THE CREW WAS BACK in their hideout, sitting together in the main room with the massive mural of the blue whale swimming over them, the rainbow stretching over it. Wyatt couldn't quite believe this was what his life had led to. A couple of weeks ago, he never would have imagined he would be traveling the world with an old flame, rekindling the fire between them while on a wild scavenger hunt leading to a life-changing amount of money. If someone had told him what was in his future, he likely would have laughed and asked which asylum they broke free from.

But it *was* his life. And he was quickly adjusting to it. In the beginning of this adventure, he was swimming in doubt and feeling like an outsider. But now? He felt like one of the Rainbow's Seven; he felt like he had earned his spot. It was an exhilarating sensation, as if he were standing on top of the world. Nothing could knock him off. He had his man, he had his crew, and soon, he'd have his money.

Nothing could ruin this for him.

Wyatt sat next to Doc, chatting about their favorite books as Roman set up the space for their last rundown before tomorrow's job. He was finding himself opening up more and more to the slightly sarcastic and incredibly intelligent Doc, with her penchant for reading some extra-smutty historicals with a straight face.

"Book or movie? Which do you usually like?" Wyatt asked, grabbing a strawberry from the bowl on his lap and taking a juicy bite.

"Book, for sure. Movie *sometimes*, but it has to be exceptionally well done. I want them to pluck the scenes directly from my twisted little psyche."

"Agree, agree." Wyatt tipped the bowl in her direction. "Want some?"

"Sure. I don't think anyone can say no to fresh strawberries."

"Except maybe my mom. She was allergic to them. Like deathly allergic."

Doc's thin brows rose. "Oh damn, that's a tough allergy. I'm fine with peanut and, like, horse allergies? But come at my cats, my berries, or my flowers, and then I'm pissed."

Wyatt chuckled, getting another mouthful of

The Sunset Job

strawberry and washing it down with some rosé. "Also agree."

"Speaking of parents, Salt... I never got to finish the story I was telling you on the plane."

Wyatt nodded, not having forgotten their small heart-to-heart but also not wanting to press, either. He wasn't drunk enough for that.

"It's not a great one, I'll just start there. And it kind of ties into why I'm here. Then again, don't our parents tie into the reason why we're *all* here?" Doc shrugged and gave a sad little giggle. "It started with my dad—my inspiration and my everything, really. I wanted to be just like him. And he was so proud of me, knowing that I wanted to follow in his footsteps, becoming a renowned surgeon rolling in money and respect. Like father, like child.

"You can imagine how upset he became when I told him I was trans. It was as if I came home and told him I'd killed ten people at the supermarket. Like the world was ending. Like it was the hardest thing he could ever have to endure, never once thinking about how hard it was for *me*. How badly I needed him to hold me and hug me and say he'll love me no matter what. *That's* the proper response, and nothing else will ever suffice."

"Oh, Doc, fuck. I'm so sorry." Wyatt's heart immediately felt a thousand pounds heavier. His coming-out story wasn't anything like Doc's; his parents had followed the exact script she wished her dad had.

"Yeah. I was nineteen at this point, so I left home. Found a group of people that would take me in and found happiness within that. Except, I knew there was more to my journey before I considered it complete. I knew I wanted gender reassignment surgery but also knew I had no way to pay for it. I saved up the little I got from my two jobs, but it didn't cut it. So I got what I saved and went to gamble it: first on blackjack, then I tried craps and then fell into poker. In a few nights, I had done it, and I was on an all-new high." Doc softly dropped her head back against the wall behind the couch they were sitting on. "That's when the rest of my problems started. I started to lose, and I kept losing, and losing and losing. And I tried taking out a loan from a sketchy source, lost that. Went to another, lost that. You get the picture. I owe some really bad people a whole lot of money."

"That's okay, Doc. That's why we're working this job, so that all our lives can change. I've got your back. We all do."

She smiled, and Wyatt was surprised to see a few tears slip from her brown eyes.

"Thank you, Salt. You're a good guy. A really good one. I'm glad Roman has you."

The weight on his heart lifted slightly, replaced by the warmth that radiated off Doc's smile. She gave

The Sunset Job

Wyatt a friendly shoulder bump before taking another strawberry.

"Seriously, though, your mom is missing out."

Wyatt was about to correct the tense, something he'd sadly gotten used to since their passing, but was stopped by a slight commotion at the front of the room.

It was Roman and Bang Bang, working to set up the projector and dimming the lights. Time for their rundown on tomorrow's last leg. There'd be plenty of time after to have some more heart-to-hearts with his new bestie.

"Alright, everyone settled in?" Roman asked, looking around at the assembled six. He stood in front of the group, wearing a fitted navy T-shirt and a pair of gray gym shorts that did a terrible job of hiding his VPL (which Wyatt was quite grateful for). He pulled his gaze up from the mouthwatering outline and focused on what Roman had to say next.

"This is it, ladies and gents. We're in the home stretch. The job is almost finished, and all that'll be left is us riding off into the sunset together. We just have to grab the tome, and we're set." He dimmed the lights and turned on the projector, the wall filling with a photo of the Broad, a museum in Los Angeles made to look like a building in motion and lovingly called the Cheese Grater by local Angelinos. "Our target is in this building, set for a months-long exhibition on famous literature throughout the years.

Unfortunately, because of the last failed attempt at grabbing the book, the museum has upped security, making things slightly more complicated this time around."

"What did they implement for security?" Mimic asked, a small black notebook in her hand and the end of her pen between her teeth.

"There's two armed guards by the entrance to the exhibit at all times, along with a swarm of cameras and alarms surrounding the tome. When the museum closes at night, the tome is moved into a secure vault that would be even harder to get through. I doubt the museum managers even understand why all the security, but it doesn't matter. It's something we have to deal with."

"And how will we do that?" Mustang asked, arms crossed against her chest, covering the band logo on her T-shirt.

"We have an important inside connection at the museum." Roman's gaze turned to Phantom, who had a bandage wrapped around his chest, a backward cap thrown on his head with a matching pair of black sweats. "Phantom's sister, Alecia, works as one of the museum's curators. She should be able to walk us right up to the tome. We'll be going in during the middle of the day, when the museum is busiest. Salt, you'll need to get into the system and throw the cameras on some kind of loop, along with knocking out the alarm system so we can get out clean."

The Sunset Job

"Got it," Wyatt said, feeling a surge of adrenaline flood through him. It sounded easy enough but entirely depended on just how much of the museum's budget had gone to cybersecurity. Wyatt assumed just about as much as what went into landscaping.

"Then we turn to Phantom's sister. She likely won't be able to open the glass and take out the tome without security saying something, so Mimic and Bang Bang, you two will create a distraction up front. Draw security to you."

They both nodded, the two sharing an almost comical fist bump, Bang Bang's fist eclipsing Mimic's.

"Of course, we need to consider the Pride, since they've seemed to predict almost all of our moves. Everyone needs to be armed and ready. We want to do this quietly, but if it gets loud, then it gets loud." Roman clicked through some photos of the museum, showing various entrance and exit points, highlighting areas that could serve as ambush spots, blind spots. He appeared to be covering nearly every base, but Wyatt could tell there was still some opaqueness to his information and directives. He wasn't giving the exact time or day of their operation and dodged a couple of questions from Doc about his thoughts on *how* the Pride knew their almost every move.

Wyatt understood—he could sense the subtle suspicion that undoubtedly slipped into Roman's consciousness. It may not have been the best time or place to express that, but Wyatt could sense it regardless.

And so could the others. The mood soured after Mustang made an icy comment about the lack of trust Roman was showing. "We've been through way too much shit for you to be playing this game, Roman."

"I'm not the one playing a game here. The Pride has their ears on what we're doing, and part of my job leading you all is keeping you all safe, and that means making sure the Pride can't hear shit. I'm not hiding anything vital to—"

"You're not even telling us *the day*, Roman." Mustang's voice raised slightly. Mimic put an arm around her shoulder, but Mustang shook it off. "Trust is what drives me, and to know you don't trust us is like a slap across the face. None of us here would work with Leonidas, like come on now. How can you even insinuate something like that."

"Shh, baby, it's okay."

"No, Mimic, it's really not. Do you like the suggestion that you're working with someone as monstrous as Leonidas? Huh? No, I didn't think so. How about you, Bang Bang? Phantom? Doc?" She turned to Wyatt, his mouth drying as if she dumped a bag of sand into it. "Salt?" He didn't respond, didn't even blink. He could feel her anger rising and was scared that this might all somehow unravel, right when they were about to cross the finish line.

"None of us are working for that fucking shit-bag." Mustang stood, fists bundled at her sides. "And the fact that you think so fucking hurts."

Roman was about to speak but was cut off by a furious Mustang. "You all can call a fucking Uber. I'm out."

She stormed past Roman, disappearing through two ocean-blue double doors, leaving the rest of the Rainbow's Seven in a stunned kind of silence, only broken by the rustle of clothes as Mimic stood and followed Mustang's smoke trail.

Chapter 26

Roman Ashford

THIS WAS the last thing Roman needed before going to steal the tome. He needed his crew working like a fine-tuned machine, well-oiled and efficient. Any cracks in their foundation could easily spread, turning what he previously assumed to be concrete into quicksand. Mustang's anger could spread like a virus, ratcheting up tension and weakening the bonds between them.

He couldn't have that. Roman needed to be a leader; he had to talk to Mustang and get her to see his point of view.

It was late, but some sunlight still clung to the evening sky, giving the aquarium an odd twilight-zone kind of feel. He walked past the empty cafeteria, through Amphibian Alley, where the *ribbits* competed with the crickets, past the Seal Sea, where

The Sunset Job

a couple of night keepers were currently having a mini training session with a few seals, none of them acknowledging Roman as he continued on.

He knew where Mustang and Mimic would be. There was one place she had always loved more than others.

And Roman was right. He walked through the snowcapped tunnel that led into Beluga Bay, where an entire observation auditorium had been built for guests to sit and watch the five beluga whales swim around them, playing with the various different enrichment toys that were dropped in and swapped out every other day. The air inside the auditorium was set to reflect the cool temperatures of the water, hitting Roman in the face with a cold blast of air as he entered.

Mimic and Mustang were sitting on the frontmost bench as two belugas, Daphne and Fred, tossed a red ribbon between them, using their tail fins to pass the ribbon to each other, their white folds shimmering under the blue light that filtered through the water. Like plump mermaids from some other planet. Mustang wasn't the only one who loved these hypnotizing creatures.

"Now, watch Fred go taunt Velma with the ribbon," Roman said as he sat down next to Mustang. Sure enough, the beluga whale with the red ribbon between his teeth swam at a much smaller beluga, running the ribbon all across the beluga's face before letting it go and swimming off. "He's been doing that for a while now. Might have a crush on her."

"Maybe," Mustang said, eyes on the wall of glass.

"I'll leave you two alone," Mimic said as she stood, hand still holding Mustang's. She kissed it before letting go. The taps of her shoes against the smooth floor followed her out.

"I'm sorry—"

"I'm sorry—"

The dual apologies came at the same time. Roman smiled and forged ahead, wanting to explain himself first. "I trust you, Mustang. Enough to put all of our lives on the line while you whip us through cramped streets. I trust you to have my back, and I hope you trust me to have yours. I would be a shitty-ass leader if I didn't trust you, but also if I didn't want to keep you all safe. And that means taking some extra precautions with information. It could be complete bullshit, and I could be overreacting, but the Pride has their ear on us somehow. With us being almost done, I don't want to take a single chance."

Mustang pushed a thick curl of brown hair behind her ear, a row of silver earrings catching the light. "I get that. I do, boss." She leaned back, looking up at the shimmering water, three of the belugas swimming past them in a straight line. "I let my anger and, well, my pride get the best of me. I did. I went straight to nuclear mode... I just can't imagine ever working alongside the devil himself, so it hurt to think you saw that."

"I'm sorry," Roman repeated. "You know the world we play in doesn't always follow logic and rules. It makes things harder to predict."

"I understand," Mustang said. "And I trust you, Roman. Whatever you've got planned, I'll follow along without any more questions."

"No, I *want* the questions. I'm not a god—I don't want to make you all think my word is the final say. I have my own blind spots. I make mistakes. But together, we can usually get over most of the speed bumps."

"Only if I'm the one driving."

"Of course."

Mustang bumped her shoulder into Roman's. She nodded toward the exit. "Should we get back to the gang? Before they think I'm drowning you in the shark exhibit?"

Roman nodded, laughing as they both stood up. Mustang waved goodbye at her beluga pals, and the two of them walked back to the hideout, joking about the beluga whales and how they might deserve a cut from the pot after all the emotional support they'd provided.

Entering the hideout, they were greeted with loud music and Bang Bang gathering everyone up in the center of the room. He spotted them and waved them over, the sour mood from earlier no longer spoiling their night. Everyone was smiling, drinking, laughing. It was like one of those tacky "live, laugh, love" posters but in real life.

"Alright, gang, everyone pair up." Bang Bang took center stage as he looked around the room, holding two boxes in both his hands. One was a game of Twister, and the other looked like a case meant to hold hundreds of dollars. "We're playing Drag Twister tonight, *brokis*."

"Drag Twister?" Phantom asked, sitting up on the couch. He no longer winced when he made movements, making Roman confident that he'd heal up in no time, thanks mostly in part to the miracle worker that was Doc.

"Drag Twister, sí. I made it up, but it's simple: one person spins the Twister wheel, and whatever body part and color that lands is what you use to make-up your partner, after all the foundation goes on."

"Right, obviously," Phantom said, likely not knowing the difference between foundation for a building and foundation for a face.

"There's some wigs in that box over there. Then, once we're all in our doll forms, we play actual Twister. Sounds fun, right? And don't worry, no one has to tuck tonight." Bang Bang looked around the room like an eager puppy waiting for a peanut-butter-filled treat.

"Tucking? What's that?" Phantom asked.

"It's when you turn your downstairs into an invisible upstairs," Mustang said, smirking.

"That's... actually a pretty good description," Bang Bang said. His hands went to the zipper on his shorts. "I can demonstrate if you—"

"No need, no need," Phantom said with a chuckle. "I think I got it."

"Good deal," Bang Bang said. He set down the two boxes, opening up the larger one to reveal a well-organized display of different makeup products.

"Sounds like a blast," Wyatt said, clapping as he stood up. "I call the blonde wigs. I think that'll look better on my skin."

The rest of the crew devolved into laughter and chatter as they scattered into partners and plotted out their makeup plans. Roman and Wyatt paired off, starting the game by having to paint each other's faces with their feet.

Needless to say, none of them came out looking their best that night, but they also ended up having one of their best nights ever, the bond between the Rainbow's Seven cementing even further under a haze of terrible makeup applications and shake-and-go wigs that made them all look like they'd robbed a Party City.

Things are going to be alright.

Roman thought as the night wound down, the crew beginning to stretch and yawn. He had an unshakeable confidence that the rest of their road would be smooth.

Unfortunately, for Roman, confidence didn't equate to fortune-telling.

* * *

Roman decided to spend the night in his condo, not far from the aquarium but slightly more comfortable for him. He was back in his bedroom, having washed off the makeup and changed into a pair of boxers, ready to climb into bed and get the next day started. Tomorrow would bring them either wild success or devastating failure; Roman understood there wasn't an in-between. If everything went according to plan, then the seven of them would be some of the richest people on the planet by nightfall, able to go anywhere and do anything. Like plugging in a cheat code and coming up with unlimited funds.

And it wasn't all about Roman's bank account, either. He was already set, with a big enough cushion to last him a couple of years of rainy days. But he knew that each one of the Rainbow's Seven needed that money for different reasons—*that* was what drove him forward. Yes, never having to work another job again was a great motivator, but providing for his crew just hit different.

Roman got into bed, dimming the lights and sitting back on the cushioned headboard, arms behind his head. Miami Beach glittered and twinkled to his right, through the floor-to-ceiling windows that turned his bedroom into a gallery.

He looked toward the bathroom, where the sound of the shower turned to a trickle. Yes, he was excited about tomorrow, but there was still the matter of tonight and the fact that a freshly washed and smiling Wyatt just stepped out of his bathroom, towel wrapped loosely around his hips, a happy trail of light brown hair leading down toward a bulge in the towel.

"God, that rainfall showerhead should be illegal. I don't know why, but it should. It's just too perfect."

Roman laughed, drinking Wyatt's lithe body up like a glass of only the finest whiskey. The soft orange light painted him in pure gold, highlighting the dip of his chest, the curve of his hips, the pebbled buds on his chest.

"Is that why you were in there for ten hours?" Roman teased.

"I was not."

"Sorry, eleven."

"Yeah, that sounds about right," Wyatt said with a chuckle as he went over to the pair of shorts he'd left out.

"Hold up," Roman said. "Leave those there."

"But I didn't bring any pajamas."

"And?"

Wyatt must have picked up on the hungry glare reflected in Roman's light green eyes. The bulge in the towel twitched. He grabbed the bundled-up edge and untied it, turning as he took it off, revealing the most perfect bubble butt Roman had ever laid eyes on. Round and firm and mouthwateringly thick. Roman felt like he could never get tired of that view. It was a view that even won over the inky expanse of stars that stretched out over the ocean, a distant cluster of storm clouds lighting up the sky with bright and persistent flashes of lightning.

"Get over here," Roman said, deciding he wasn't going to be the only one wearing clothes. He pulled off his boxers and dropped them on the floor. Wyatt's eyes fell to Roman's growing cock, already thick against his thigh. "We've got a lot to get done tonight."

"Oh, really?" Wyatt said mischievously. He held himself in his hands as he walked over to the side of the bed, moving a hand over to Roman's chest, rubbing the strong muscles. "I thought tonight was supposed to be chill."

"It's going to be everything but chill," Roman said, growling as he grabbed Wyatt by the hips and pulled him onto the bed. Wyatt straddled Roman, their growing lengths rubbing together as they locked themselves in a kiss.

Tomorrow would undoubtedly bring change in one way or another, but all Roman cared about was *tonight* and the inevitable bliss that would come with it.

Chapter 27

Wyatt Hernandez

Wyatt was horny. The lusty kind of horny that blurred the edges of his vision and made the beating of his heart loud enough to be heard from next door. Thirsty. Hungry. Desperate for Roman, desperate to get his hands and body all over the hunk of muscle wearing a cocky grin.

Knowing how empty and boring his life had been during Roman's absence only made moments like these burn hotter.

"Mhmm, you smell good." Roman leaned in and took a deep whiff, burying his nose in Wyatt's neck and coming back with a lick, his tongue sending a jolt of electricity down toward his already rock-hard cock.

"It's whatever soap you've got in there. The eucalyptus one."

"That's shampoo."

"Well, I've got hair on my body, don't I?"

Roman laughed and kissed the spot of dark hair growing on Wyatt's chest, licking there, too. Wyatt couldn't help but grind down on Roman, their legs twining together as their twitching lengths rubbed, Wyatt feeling a trail of wet warmth tracing a line from his hip to his belly. He reached down and grabbed Roman in his hand, closing around the velvety-soft skin, groaning with how heavy and firm he felt.

"Lay down," Roman said. "I want to use a toy on you."

This got Wyatt's engine revved to turbo, making him ready to burst. He ate up Roman's muscular form as he got up from the bed and walked over to his closet, his ass bouncing with every step, walking into the closet empty-handed and coming out of it with a few interesting items.

"And here I was thinking you were going to bring out the Tonka trucks."

Roman chuckled, the sound low and deep. "No, definitely not. I don't think you want one of those up your ass."

"This is true," Wyatt said, feeling a complete sense of comfort with Roman, elevating this night in ways he hadn't imagined. The room, full of modern furniture and abstract artwork, began to take on a dreamlike effect, like it had all been painted by some surrealist painter. The pinks and purples and blues from the bars, restaurants, and clubs on Ocean Drive twinkled up at them like tiny stars through the window.

This has to be a dream. Logic can't explain this moment.

"Here, let's try this one first." Roman laid the toys down on the bed, holding on to the purple silicone anal beads. He opened his nightstand drawer and took out the lube, hypnotizing Wyatt with every step.

"Ever used anal beads before?" Roman asked as he got back onto the bed.

Wyatt shook his head, eyes moving from the toy to Roman's leaking cock. "I've never used anything before. Just me and Mr. Hand... and a banana peel once. That just got really messy, though."

Roman chuckled, setting the toy down and rubbing Wyatt's legs, spreading them apart on the bed. "Beats out the time I cut a hole into a watermelon and almost got my dick stuck inside."

"That happened to you?"

"Yes, yes it did. I had forgotten I could *naturally* make myself smaller, though. Thankfully, no one had to call the fire department to saw out my dick from a melon." He ran his hands over Wyatt's hard length, then back down, cupping both his balls and giving them a gentle massage before moving further, sliding between Wyatt's cheeks.

"Nothing's getting stuck tonight, right?" Wyatt

The Sunset Job

asked playfully. He lifted himself off the bed and gave Roman some more access.

"Nothing that shouldn't, no."

Wyatt was about to ask what *should* but quickly lost track of his thoughts when Roman pressed the lubed-up end of the anal beads up against him. He relaxed into it as the first bead went in, his hole clenching around the toy.

"Fuck," Roman let out with a breathy sigh. "How's that feel?"

"Like I need more."

Roman licked his lips, the smirk turning into an O as he watched three more progressively larger beads disappear inside of Wyatt. He reached down and grabbed Wyatt's cock while he swirled the beads, causing Wyatt's back to arch and his toes to curl. The beads were deep, pressing against parts of him that tightened his core and made his cock drip with a clear string of precome, pooling just underneath his belly button. Roman took it on his thumb and brought it up to his lips, eyes locked with Wyatt as he sucked on his own finger and drank him up.

"Mhmm, seems like you like this, don't you?"

He could only nod and flash puppylike eyes at Roman as he pushed in another bead, the largest one of the set. Wyatt sucked in a breath, letting himself feel every piece of this moment, allowing every sensation to sink in deeper and deeper. He let his head fall back onto the plush pillow as Roman played with his body, stroking and kissing while slowly twirling the beads inside of him.

"How does this feel?"

Roman pulled one of the beads out, Wyatt's eyes popping open even wider. He then tugged out another, then another. Wyatt's hold tightened around each one, his body already crying out for more.

"So fucking good," Wyatt managed to say, just as Roman pushed the beads back in.

"Good," Roman said, leaning back with a devilish grin. "Now it's my turn."

Wyatt leaned up, the beads pushing harder against his sensitive prostate, his cock twitching with pleasure.

"This one's a vibrating plug," Roman said, grabbing the black silicone toy and pressing a button on the base, the hum of the vibrations filling the room. "I want you to use it on me."

Wyatt didn't need any more coaxing than that. He grabbed the plug and squirted some lube on it and on Roman, who already had his legs lifted in the air. Wyatt set the slippery bottle down on the floor and spread the lube around Roman with his fingers, sliding one in and eliciting a delicious moan from the man, his six-pack rippling with pleasure. His tattoo of the snake and dagger moved as if it were actually real, and by Roman's increasingly loud grunts, Wyatt could tell not much prep would be needed.

The Sunset Job

"Ready?" Wyatt asked, taking his finger out and replacing it with the tip of the toy, the vibrations set to Off.

Roman nodded, his bottom lip pale from how hard his bite on it was. Seeing him like this, legs in the air and ass exposed, all for Wyatt, it had the equivalent effect of dropping a truck full of lit fireworks directly into his chest. He lubed the vibrator and pushed it in, Roman instantly thrusting out his hands to stop him from going any further.

"Whoa, fuck, okay. Go," he said, releasing his grip. Wyatt pushed the vibrator in deeper, finding less and less resistance, Roman's body showing how hungry he was for it, how hard it made him.

With the entire plug inside, Wyatt pressed on the power button. Roman's entire body convulsed as the vibrations rocked through his core, his hands searching for something to grip on the bed, finding only bundles of the comforter. Wyatt turned it off, allowing a moment for Roman to catch his breath.

"Fuck, that was intense. Do it again."

The writhing returned, Roman's mouth turning into the shape of a perfect circle, his eyes rolling back as he fisted his cock, holding it tight. Wyatt leaned down and sucked on his nipple, causing him to buck up. "Fuck!" Roman said. "Fuck, fuck."

They played like that for what could have been minutes or hours, Wyatt wasn't really sure. Time lost all meaning, the world fading away along with all of its problems and worries, leaving only their flushed bodies behind.

"I want to fuck you," Roman said, grabbing Wyatt's hips and flipping him over. "While you use that remote to control the vibrator."

Wyatt reached over for the remote, stopping short as Roman began to pull out the beads, the first one out being the largest and the last one coming out with ease. He grabbed the remote off the nightstand and got back on his hands and knees, back arched and ass out. Roman grabbed both lobes of muscle, squeezing and spreading them before spreading more lube in between, some of it trailing down Wyatt's already tightening balls.

"Ready for me?" Roman asked, lining himself up.

"Are you ready for *me*?" Wyatt looked over his shoulder, kissing the top of the remote with a lusty smile on his freckled face.

Roman pushed in, and Wyatt nearly forgot all about the remote, his head dropping and a moan escaping his lips as he stretched to accommodate the thick man.

"My turn," Wyatt said, his grin turning into another O-shaped moan as Roman thrust forward. He found a rhythm immediately, but Wyatt wasn't about to make it *that* easy for him. He pressed on the "2," turning the vibrator on at the medium level and throwing Roman's rhythm right off. His fingers dug into Wyatt's hips, his cock still filling him, the buzz from his ass traveling all the way into Wyatt's.

"*Fuuuck,*" Roman groaned, pulling out before thrusting back in, the vibrator still doing its job. Wyatt's eyes rolled back, the dick game hitting a home-fucking-run. He looked down, realizing he'd created a mini puddle underneath them from all the precome he was leaking.

Wyatt pressed on the "3," and Roman started to thrust as if there was an earthquake rocking through the entire condo building. "Ohhhh, gah damn, fuck." Roman was nearly intelligible, causing Wyatt to laugh, which then spread to Roman. Soon, the two men were leaking and vibrating and fucking *laughing*.

No logical explanation for it, and Wyatt couldn't care less.

He dropped his head as Roman kissed the back of his neck, the laughter diminishing, leaving only the sound of skin slapping against skin mixing with the buzz of the vibrator.

"I'm so close, baby."

"Me too," Wyatt said, feeling his every muscle tighten, the impending wave of ecstasy cresting just over the horizon.

"Do it, Wyatt. Come for me. Let me fuck it out of you."

Wyatt's moan turned loud, animalistic, urging Roman on with "yes, please, more, *more!*" And he blew, the orgasm shredding through him, his cock shooting out ropes of come onto the sheets, his legs shaking and his hole twitching with every shot.

Roman's climax wasn't far behind at all. He bucked into Wyatt, burying himself deep and shooting his load, coating Wyatt's insides, claiming him, making him his. He bent over and sucked Wyatt's neck between his teeth, clamping down, his cock still going.

It was nearly otherworldly. Wyatt had to take a couple of deep breaths once they separated, slowing down his heart before it ended up exploding just like they had.

Everything was bright, even though it was the middle of the night. Colors popped, light shone, framed art seemed to come to life.

"Come, let's clean up," Roman said, grabbing Wyatt's hand and leading him to the bathroom. There, they washed up, kissing and teasing and chuckling, the bliss that coursed through their veins making it hard to form long and coherent sentences. They went back to bed, where Roman changed out the comforter for one that wasn't drenched with Wyatt's come. They got back into bed, both of them spent in the best way possible.

And then it happened. Like lightning out of a clear blue sky, striking without any warning, hitting the ground and creating a fiery explosion.

"I love you, Salt, with everything I've got inside

The Sunset Job

me," Roman said, looking deep into Wyatt's eyes, leaving no doubt that he meant the words he was saying. "Every cell, every inch of my soul. I love you, and I always have. I was just scared to ever say it out loud, but not anymore. Never again. I love you."

Wyatt melted into the words, his body forming a blissful little puddle around Roman. He couldn't believe he was hearing those words after years of wondering what they'd sound like and years of trying to forget all about them. He'd been angry at Roman, more so than he'd ever been with anyone else. Wyatt's entire life trajectory had been altered because of a bad decision led by the man with arms wrapped around him. He had sworn to himself to keep Roman at arm's length, thinking that would somehow put out the flames that still roared between them.

So much for arm's length.

Wyatt kissed Roman's chest before shifting back so that he could look into Roman's eyes, the soft bedroom lighting creating a golden-green illusion to them.

"Roman, I..." Wyatt became choked with a surprise burst of emotion, his words having to work to get through. "I love you, too, Roman. I really do."

They kissed again and smiled and kissed and whispered more "I love you's," like they were kids again, just learning the power of the world, experiencing the rush of sparkles and warmth, wanting it to never end.

"Life is going to be a dream after tonight," Roman said during a break in their affection. "We can have a date night in Bali and another in Santorini. Watch a movie in London and have dinner in Italy so I could take you up to our penthouse suite where I could devour you until the sun comes up. We can choose to do anything, go anywhere. And we get to experience it all together."

"Life already feels like a dream." Wyatt decided to be honest. Vulnerability never came easy to him, but that had changed now that he'd opened his heart back up to Roman.

"Just you wait, Salt. It's only going to get better from here on out."

"I can't even imagine how," he said. "Everything you said obviously sounds incredible, but I already feel *so* freaking happy. Insanely so. And I wasn't expecting it, either. I really thought I'd have a harder time getting over things."

More honesty, more truth. Wyatt wanted to lay it all out. He wanted to be as naked as his skin was.

He continued, rolling over so Roman's arm was under his head, his gaze tilted up at the dark ceiling. "I'm not great with letting go of grudges, you know that. But I'm kind of realizing that I never really had a grudge toward you. Not in the way I thought I had. There wasn't any hate or anger or resentment being aimed toward you... it was just sadness. Sad that things fell apart, sad that we didn't work out, sad that my life was turning out the way it was. And then I became full of questions, not just the whys or the what-ifs, but 'how is he?' and 'is he okay?'"

"Salt, you're shredding my heart with a chainsaw."

"It's okay, you don't have to feel bad or anything. Saying this is like tossing it all in a box and throwing it in a fire. It helps, it really does."

"If I could turn back—"

"You don't have to turn anything back," Wyatt said, propping himself up on an elbow so he could look down into Roman's crystalized green orbs. He could stare into those eyes for the rest of eternity, finding a new facet to love about them with every day that passed.

"Thank you, Salt. For taking me back, for coming with me. I've built up a lot of scar tissue from people hurting me in my past, and I really don't think I would have let anyone in, not after I felt like I lost the love of my life." Roman took Wyatt's hand and kissed each of his fingers. "But I've found him again, and I don't need to let anyone else in as deep as I've let you."

Tingles swirled through each of Wyatt's fingers as Roman's soft lips pressed against them. If he shut his eyes, he could imagine the plump white comforters underneath him turning into fluffy clouds, carrying the two men off into the sunset.

"I wonder what Angie and Scott are going to think about us getting back together," Wyatt mused, thinking back to their two closest high school friends. He still spoke to them every now and then, their friendship being the kind that always bounced back after a quick conversation, no matter how much time had passed since the last one.

"Angie is probably going to laugh nervously and say something about how she always saw it coming, and Scott would slap us on our asses and say congratulations."

"That's actually—yeah, I think that's on point."

Roman put both hands behind his head and crossed his feet, his eyes somewhere around Wyatt's lips. "When's the last time you spoke to them?"

"A couple months, I think. You?"

"Years," Roman said, expression dropping slightly. Wyatt didn't want that, not tonight.

"We'll have a mini reunion when this is all over," he said, lying back down with his head on Roman's chest. "What's going to be the first thing you want to do once we have the tome?"

"Kiss you."

"Obviously."

"And lick, and suck, and most definitely fu—"

"Got it. *After* all that," Wyatt said, glad that they were already on the same page.

The Sunset Job

"After I turn you into a sweaty, shaky, come-drenched mess—"

"Nice, very romantic—"

"—I'll bring you into the shower, wash you off, kiss every part of you all over again." Roman kissed Wyatt's head. "And then I'll make sure you and Julie are set up, make sure you two never have to worry about a damn thing. Then I'll take you to our new home in..." Roman cocked his head, eyebrow arching.

"Are you looking for suggestions?"

"Yeah, obviously. It's you and me from here on out, Salt."

Wyatt liked the sound of that. They stayed up talking for another hour, going over their dream countries to live in, narrowing down potential beach homes and mountainside cabins and city-center high-rises. Wyatt still had a difficult time believing it all wasn't a dream, even when sleep did finally overtake him.

Chapter 28

Roman Ashford

THIS WAS IT. Today was the day they'd all been waiting for. The final stretch of their job, the finish line they were all salivating to cross.

The flight from Miami to LA wasn't as celebratory as the one prior. They were silent this time around, sans champagne or cramped bathroom hookups. Instead, everyone was going over the plan, asking questions, poking holes, suggesting fixes, and trying to be as best prepared as they could be.

Roman did his best with keeping everyone on the same page. He sat next to Wyatt for the entire six-hour flight, holding his hand for most of it.

"You feeling okay?" Roman asked as they started their descent into LAX.

"I just can't believe it's all over after today."

"Don't think of it like that. Think of it like being a new beginning after today."

The Sunset Job

Wyatt smiled, his cheeks rising and carrying those dimples with them. Roman was sure that if he were held at gunpoint and asked to recreate Wyatt's freckles, he'd be able to do it with his eyes closed. He loved the little marks on either side of his face, perfectly symmetrical and perfectly Wyatt.

Once off the plane, the Rainbow's Seven went directly to the bathrooms, where the crew changed into their outfits. Roman and Wyatt both walked out, having swapped their sweats for suits, Roman ironing out a wrinkle from his maroon tie, the silver clip catching the white airport lights.

"You look good," Wyatt said, eyes going from Roman's shining leather wingtips and up to his styled hair, which had grown out since his last haircut.

"And you look great, Salt." Roman took a step back so he could properly appreciate the look. Mimic had somehow managed to get them tailored Gucci suits for the job in less time than it took for an Amazon delivery, explaining that her museum curators were going to be the best-damn-looking curators on this side of the globe.

And she wasn't lying. Wyatt immediately fit in with the Los Angeles crowd, appearing vaguely recognizable and ambiguously famous in his ironed-out three-piece suit. His silk tie—a bright violet color — popped off the light pink-and-purple shirt he wore, small floral designs adding an extra layer of life to the shirt. He had on a pair of impenetrably dark Ray-

Bans, which he lifted up and winked from underneath.

Roman couldn't take it, not kissing him. He grabbed Wyatt's elbows and pulled him in tight, his lips homing in like missiles, locking around Wyatt's. He wrapped his arms around him, loving how it felt when they were tight around Wyatt. It was like he held the entire sun against him, infusing him with a heat strong enough to create life and destroy planets.

When they separated, Roman found himself smiling from ear to ear, the pre-job nerves he'd usually get nowhere to be found.

"Hey, question," Wyatt asked while they waited for the others. "Why don't you have a nickname? Everyone's got one but you."

Roman leaned against the wall, unable to stop eating up Wyatt with his eyes. The man could really pull off a suit, same as he could pull off wearing just a pair of glasses and some boxers. "I've never had one stick," he answered with a shrug. Mustang and Mimic came out of the bathrooms to join them just then, Mimic in a casual pair of jeans and black spaghetti-strap tank and Mustang in a pair of shredded jean shorts and an Avengers T-shirt, sleeves rolled all the way up so the black mamba tattoo going up her left arm was in full view.

"Besides Mustang calling me 'Assfuck,' I've never had one that fit more than just Roman."

"Nicknames?" Mustang asked, Wyatt nodding in

response. "Oh yeah, this one's only ever Roman or Assfuck, depending on how annoyed I am with him."

"Roman's a pretty badass name anyway," Wyatt said. There was a twinkle in his gaze, and seeing it threw Roman right back to the day in the Miami Science Museum, when all this had just started. Wyatt had looked terrified back then but also pissed the fuck off. There wasn't a light in his eyes back then, only swirling darkness, all of it directed at Roman.

There was none of that anymore. Wyatt looked up into Roman's eyes with love pouring out of his. It's what had made it so easy for Roman to say those three little words the night before. He'd had no fears that Wyatt wouldn't say it back, because he'd already been saying it with his eyes, telling a story that Roman knew he'd never grow tired of reading.

The crew was complete when Bang Bang, Phantom, and Doc joined them, only Bang Bang having changed from his sweatpants into a pair of dark jeans and a white T-shirt, a leather jacket thrown over. Phantom and Doc would be holding things down in their hotel, so both had stayed wearing their comfortable travel clothes. With everyone assembled and ready, Roman led the Rainbow's Seven out of the airport and to the parking lot, where a Mercedes van waited for them, the black paint shining under a cloudless LA afternoon.

They piled in, Roman taking the passenger seat

and leaning back, looking at his assembled crew. He felt confident in them, even with the minuscule cracks that had formed from the Pride's interference. There still wasn't an answer to how they were obtaining their information, and that made Roman wary, but it didn't make him distrustful. He couldn't afford any distrust between them on a day like today.

"Rainbow's Seven, you're all good with the plan?"

Roman's question was answered with a chorus of affirmations, Bang Bang's fist pounding the ceiling being the loudest of them.

"Remember, without any interference and this should be the easiest part of the job, but I can't guarantee that. Everyone needs to have their eyes and ears wide open. Second-guess everyone, double-check your surroundings, and never leave your back exposed. None of us are alone in this; we've got each other to count on, alright?"

More nods, more hoots and hollers. The adrenaline was beginning to spike, along with the volume inside the van. Tall palm trees whipped past the window as Mustang drove them down an empty residential street, the homes large and the cars expensive.

"And if I end up giving the signal to run and abort the plan, then you listen. No matter how close you think you are to the tome." Roman glanced at his

The Sunset Job

gold Rolex. Only twenty-five minutes left before they were set to rendezvous with Alecia.

Twenty-five minutes between them and limitless freedom, the tome and the key within it holding a chest full of their wildest dreams.

"Got it, Roman," Mimic said, wearing a wig with brunette waves falling down her chest, making her nearly unrecognizable. "But I don't think you've got to worry. I have a good feeling about today."

"And her 'good feelings' really mean something. We won ten thousand bucks once because she had a 'good feeling' about a casino's slot machine." Mustang blew a kiss into the rearview mirror, Mimic catching it in a delicate hand.

"We've made it this far," Phantom said. "With only one of us getting shot. That ain't too bad, right?"

"I would have preferred zero gunshot victims."

"Same," Phantom said, laughing along with the rest of the crew. The streets began to widen, and the traffic started to increase, the roads packed with cars. The Hollywood Hills rose up in the distance, dry from lack of rain but beautiful nonetheless. Roman sat back in his seat and looked out the window, catching Wyatt's reflection in the side mirror, his eyes wide and crinkled with a smile as he soaked in the views.

It made Roman excited for all the other places they could go to after this. He wanted to see the world through Wyatt's eyes, drinking in the appreciation and awe he had for everything around him. Roman had had his fair share of adventures already, so the idea of starting all brand-new ones with Wyatt made him wish he could speed up time and be done with this job.

Mustang sped up, cutting off some traffic and pulling down a busy street lined with small boutiques, windows lined with well-dressed mannequins and interesting antiques. They made another corner, Roman keeping his eyes on the rearview mirror. He knew Mustang was already making sure they weren't being tailed, but an extra pair of eyes never hurt.

So far, so good. No Pride interference. They just needed to get to the Broad, have Alecia escort them to the book, create the distraction they needed, and get the hell out of there. It was a simple plan, but in Roman's experience, simple plans unfortunately brought the messiest complications.

Chapter 29

Roman Ashford

THE BROAD LOOMED BEFORE THEM, a true oddity of a building. It reminded Roman of a storage drive for his computer, a big white angular brick of a building with "vents" built into all of its sides. The entrance was located under a triangular cutout that was made of all glass, making it feel like they were walking into the jaws of a waiting predator.

Not this time.

Roman walked with Wyatt at his side, flashing the credentials Mimic secured for them. The guards let the two in, Mimic and Bang Bang making for the regular line to buy tickets. Bang Bang gave them a subtle wink as the suited-up pair walked past them, entering a lobby made of all stone, floor to ceiling, a swirling mass of soft gray and black.

He spotted Alecia immediately, standing by a colorful art piece depicting a flock of paper birds flying upside down, a current of paper fish swimming above them, the sculpture moving with the breeze. She was holding an iPad against her light pink blouse, a matching pink headband in her hair.

Roman gave her a quick once-over. Her smile seemed easy and friendly, her eyes warm but her shoulders tense, nearly touching the white pears that dangled from her ears.

"Mr. Owens, Mr. Stevens," she said, holding a hand out.

There was a tremble there. Was she always this shaky?

Roman returned the handshake, his guard rising. "Thank you for assisting us today, Ms. Anderson."

"Of course. This *Tome of Tomorrow* exhibit has drawn a lot of eyes. I'm happy to help you bring even more to it." She led them through an administrative entrance, the heavy door shutting and blocking out all the noise from the museum. The hallway stretched ahead of them, white and bare and nothing at all like the rest of the museum.

Roman dropped his voice. "Everything okay?"

"Yes."

She walked a little faster, heels clicking on the tile. They turned a corner. Roman's hand ghosted over the holstered gun underneath his suit, every blind turn making the hair on his neck and arms stand on end. He hadn't gotten any significant signal that told him he needed to pull back, but he couldn't

The Sunset Job

deny that something about Alecia's posture, her tone, something felt off. He attributed the nerves coming from having to help them steal a valuable artifact from the place that employed her, but Roman couldn't be a hundred percent sure.

"How much farther?" he asked, Wyatt walking on the other side of Alecia.

"Just through that door. Come." The clicking of her heels went even faster. She wanted this to be done with, same as Roman. Hopefully they'd both have their wish in the next few minutes.

Alecia opened the door and let them out into a large white room, tourists filtering through different pedestals holding each of the written works in the exhibit. Roman's eyes went directly toward the *Tome of Tomorrow*, set on a center pedestal with a beaming light aimed down onto the glass case that held it. A projection of different events that Remy had predicted and written down was displayed on the far wall, directly behind the tome. People lined up to see the macabre images of the various wildfires and hurricanes he had predicted, along with a handful of shocking celebrity deaths and political disasters.

"Right this way, gentlemen."

Five security guards. All armed. Roman looked over his shoulder. *Eight security guards.*

Shit. What kind of distraction were Mimic and Bang Bang going to cause that would grab the attention of all eight of them?

"As you can see, there's a large number of security employed to make sure the tome stays safe." She gave a friendly wave toward a grim-faced security guard. The wave wasn't returned. "But aside from the guards, there's also a pressure system inside that will trigger a lockdown if it's tripped."

Roman looked to Wyatt, a quick flash of surprise crossing his face.

"That was actually added this morning."

She pulled out a key from the pocket of her white pants. "Now, I can open it for a total of five minutes before it needs to be closed again. Is that enough for your livestream?"

"Yes," Roman said, trying to ignore the dark and rotted feeling that began gnawing at his insides. He brought out his phone, looked at the time. The room was still packed with guards.

"Actually, before you open it and we flip through some of the pages, can I chat with my partner about the script?"

"Definitely. Want to go to my office?" She sounded almost relieved, like maybe Roman was suggesting an end to this before anything even happened.

"No need. We can talk here." He grabbed Wyatt's elbow and walked some steps away, out of earshot of Alecia and two of the guards.

"Did you know about the pressure alarm?" Roman asked, heart pounding.

The Sunset Job

Wyatt chewed his bottom lip before that turned into a small grin. "I did. It came up this morning when I was knocking out the rest of the security systems."

"Fuck, Salt, you're a genius. If we weren't meant to be business partners, I'd kiss you right now."

"Business partners can still kiss, can't they?"

Roman chuckled, his heart racing but his worries slightly easing. With the pressure alarm off, that meant they'd avoid the museum falling into a lockdown situation, which would have made it infinitely harder to have a clean escape with the tome.

Bang Bang's voice sounded loud in Roman's ear. "About to start the distraction, *broki*."

"Good, go. We'll see you two on the outside."

Roman nodded back toward the tome, where Alecia was looking around with big, saucer-like eyes. "Does she seem a little nervous to you?" Roman asked before they walked back to her.

"A little, but it's not exactly a regular day for her."

"No, no it's not." Roman couldn't shake it. He looked around, trying to pinpoint where the feeling of being watched was coming from. The four tourists wearing matching shirts by the corner? The lone museum visitor standing with his back to the wall, his eyes everywhere but on the exhibits? Or the husband-and-wife pair that still wore their sunglasses indoors and kept craning their heads in Roman's direction?

The walkie-talkies dangling off the hips of the guards all went off at the same time, creating an echo chamber of static and voices. One of them managed to make out the message and shouted at the rest to follow her, all eight of them apparently needed in order to handle whatever disruption Mimic and Bang Bang had just caused.

Roman and Wyatt reached Alecia's side. "Ready?" she asked, holding the key to her chest.

"Yes," Roman said. "All you need to do is open the display, and we'll grab the tome. We'll run out, and you stay behind, acting as if you were robbed. Your hands will be clean, and I'll make sure the balance in your bank account will get larger."

Alecia nodded, eyes darting over Roman's shoulder. She whispered something to herself and pushed the key into the lock. Roman held his breath. Wyatt held his hand. This was it, the tome was finally theirs—

The key didn't work. Alecia let out a frustrated breath and tried again.

"What's going on?" Roman asked, every second more vital than the last.

"It's not... This isn't the right key."

"Did they change the locks?"

"No, I don't think so. My other set of keys is in my office. I need to run back and grab them."

The Sunset Job

Roman pressed his fingers to the bridge of his nose. "How fast can you get back?"

"Minutes. Five minutes."

"Go, hurry."

She nodded, grabbing the key and bolting away, winding through a group of students trying to paint a sculpture of a mountain made out of books. Wyatt looked to Roman, wincing.

"This isn't great," he said.

"No, it isn't," Roman echoed, looking down at the tome. So close. He could take out his gun and shoot through the glass—that's all it would take to grab the tome and get out of there. But it would draw all of the attention directly to them, and Roman didn't want to risk that. Shooting a gun in a crowded museum and stealing one of the exhibits was exactly the kind of thing that would land them both in jail.

"It's fine, it's fine," Wyatt said, in a tone that sounded more like he was trying to reassure himself more than anyone else. "She'll get the right key, and we'll be out of here, that much closer—"

"No... Oh no." That's when Roman saw it. The words leaped off the page, quite literally, the message written right there, underneath the chapter heading. The curtain of realization dropped on Roman like a meteor. Realization and dread. "This isn't the tome. Salt, this isn't the real tome. Look what this chapter is titled."

Wyatt leaned in, reading the words before

reaching out for Roman's wrist, fingers clamping around him. He turned to look at Roman, shocked.

The Fall of the Rainbow's Seven

"We've been tricked. This was a setup." Roman looked to the exit, tugging Wyatt in its direction. "Bang Bang, Mimic, I need you two to abort the job. I repeat, drop whatever you're doing and get the fuck out of here. It was a trap."

Then, like an exclamation mark for his command, came two large explosions from somewhere outside, rocking the museum and breaking windows. Glass rained down, people were screaming in terror, no one knew what to do or what was going on.

No one but Roman, who understood *exactly* what was going on: he'd made another fatal mistake in underestimating the Pride, and he was about to pay a heavy price for that oversight.

Chapter 30

Wyatt Hernandez

Wyatt read the chapter heading and felt the dread seep into him like toxic vapors, filling him with every single breath. He reached for Roman. He reached for something, anything to keep his knees from giving way underneath him. This was all a setup, and they'd managed to blindly walk directly into it.

An explosion made his shoulders spasm. Another explosion made his ears ring and his stomach twist.

He looked around, panicked, devastated, terrified, trying to find the source of the explosions. People were running in all directions, grabbing their children and picking them up in their arms, crying and shouting for help.

No, no, no, no. It wasn't supposed to go like this. They had it all planned out, they had their inside connection, they had knocked out the security systems and made it all the way to the tome.

A fake Tome. The Pride had *still* got ahead of them.

"Explosion at the entrance," came Mustang's voice into Wyatt's skull. "Shit, it's bad. What the hell is going on in there?"

Mimic ran up to them, her hair a mess and her shirt tattered, as if someone had tried holding her back but ended up with only a handful of fabric. "They have Bang Bang."

"What? Who?" Roman asked, gun out of the holster and in his hands, held down by his hip.

"The police, they grabbed him. I'm sorry, Roman. I tried to get him out of there, but they almost got me." She looked to the arching doors that she'd just run in from. "They'll be here in a few minutes. We have to go."

This was worse than worst-case scenario. Wyatt couldn't allow his fear to get the better of him, not now. He needed to snap into the moment, keep his chest as high as Roman's and his expression as stoic. Surprisingly, his shoulders didn't show any signs of trembling. "Let's go that way. Alecia ran through there—I think there might be an exit out the back."

Roman tapped the earpiece. "Mustang, find your way to the back of the museum. Wherever the higher-ups park, go there. Wait for us."

"You got it."

Roman pushed Wyatt and Mimic toward the

The Sunset Job

door. "Go, get to Mustang. I'm going to see if there's anything I can do about Bang Bang."

"They had him in cuffs, Roman. We can't get to him now."

"I can at least try."

Mimic nodded, her gun now out and in her hands as well. Wyatt went for his but left it holstered, the tremble gone from his shoulders but not from his hands. They started toward the door Alecia had run through, hurrying past people who were crouched behind pedestals and sculptures. A torrent of sirens could be heard from inside the museum, the windows having been blown out. Wyatt looked back, looking for Roman—maybe he should have gone with him. Maybe if they worked together, they could rescue Bang Bang and get the hell out of there? He scanned the thinning crowd, spotting him at the far end of the room. He slipped from Mimic's grasp.

"I'm gonna try and help him."

Mimic looked like she was about to argue but suddenly froze, looking at something behind Wyatt. He turned, jaw dropping as he watched himself projected onto the wall. It was a picture of him, then of Roman, then Mimic. It was all of them, all of the Rainbow's Seven, pictured either entering the museum or surrounding it, their full legal names printed under each of the pictures. And then footage started to play, depicting masked figures entering the museum and planting the bombs, the video time-stamped as the night before. One of the masked figures had their sleeves rolled up, showing a black mamba tattoo identical to that of Mustang's.

In fact, all seven of the masked intruders on the screen resembled each of the Rainbow's Seven in size and shape. Wyatt watched as his body double reached for the *Tome of Tomorrow* after shattering the glass it was held in. The man looked directly at the camera, eyes the same color as Wyatt's. He even had on a pair of glasses over the ski mask, glasses Wyatt was sure he owned.

Another explosion tore through the wall. Mimic and Wyatt both fell to the floor. Police started to swarm into the room, guns drawn but not fully aware of who was a victim and who was hostile.

Roman came running to their side. "Let's go, hurry." He helped them back onto their feet and ran with them toward the door, opening it and lunging inside. The sterile hallway stretched ahead of them, the fluorescent lights flickering, plunging the three into a brief stretch of pure dark. One of the blasts must have taken out a generator.

"This way," Roman said, taking the lead. Wyatt followed behind with Mimic, keeping a hand on the wall to guide him when the lights went out.

"What the hell is happening?" he asked, voice tight and high.

"The Pride grabbed the book and set all this up to make us look guilty."

The Sunset Job

"But how? How did any of this happen?"

Roman could only seem to look ahead, unable to answer, his jaw clenched so that the muscles twitched under the blinking lights.

"Alecia!" Wyatt called, seeing the woman running at full speed out of her office. She ran up against the wall, looking back with intense fear reflected in her eyes. She bolted, running in the opposite direction.

"Alecia, wait!" They took off after her, the three of them racing forward, Roman proving to be the fastest of the trio. He broke ahead, gun still at his side but his shouts becoming angrier, telling Alecia to stop.

She wouldn't. She didn't even slow down. She was running from them, trying hard to outpace them.

But Roman was fast, too fast for her to lose. He caught up to her, grabbing her elbow and stopping her in her tracks, twisting her back around. She didn't struggle, only looked up into Roman's eyes with a shaky defiance, matching the tremble of her bottom lip. "I'm sorry, Roman. I had to do it. I had to do it."

"Why?" Roman asked. Wyatt felt like he had missed an entire plotline. What the hell was she talking about? What had she done? Why was she trying to run away from them?

"They had my daughter, Roman. That asshole, Leonidas, he took her. He threatened to... to—he wouldn't give her back to me unless I did what he said. And then he promised I'd have her back, and I'd have her treatment, too. I needed to do what he said. I'm so sorry."

Alecia might as well have taken a brick and smacked Wyatt across the face with it.

Shocked didn't even begin to describe it. Phantom's sister was the leak this entire time? She'd been the one helping the Pride get ahead of their every move?

A door slammed from somewhere down the hall. Footsteps echoed toward them.

"How?"

"The watch I gave to Phantom," Alecia said, tears freely flowing down her face, trailing with dark mascara that pooled under her eyelids. "It recorded everything. And last night, when you told me it was going to happen, I helped them come in and steal the tome. He didn't tell me about the bombs, though. I swear. I'm sorry."

"Jesus, Alecia." Roman let her go, rubbing a hand over his face. "You should have come to us. We would have helped."

"He said he'd kill her if I did. I couldn't go to anyone."

The footsteps grew louder, the sound of police radios growing with them.

"We have to go," Roman said, urgency bleeding into his tone. Wyatt had never seen him this panicked, and yet he had no idea how he could help. They were royally fucked, Wyatt could clearly see that.

"There isn't an exit down that way," Alecia said through more tears, throwing another wrench into the already bent-and-broken machine. If they turned and went the way they came, then they'd run head-first into a mini battalion of LAPD officers. Alecia grabbed the ring of keys and grabbed a large silver one, running to another door.

"Through here. Break through the window—that should put you in the Renaissance Hall. If you go straight through and make a left, you should find an exit."

Roman grabbed the key, uttering a tiny thanks as he unlocked the door and threw it open. The three of them ran inside the office, where two employees cowered underneath the desk. They didn't have any time for explanations or apologies. Roman grabbed an office chair and hurled it at the glass window, sending shards of glass flying into the Renaissance Hall.

Roman helped Wyatt and Mimic get through the broken window and over the broken glass, following right behind them. Some of the glass must have cut up his palm, leaving thin streaks of bright red blood.

"This way," he said, grabbing Wyatt's hand, seemingly unaware of whatever injuries he might have had. They ran through rows and rows of classic paintings, the people inside appearing to follow them with their oil-painted eyes.

"There! Freeze!"

The shouts came from behind them, spurring them on. They took the left turn and found themselves in a dimly lit hallway, a rare collection of gemstones and crystals displayed in the walls. Directly ahead of them was a blinking red exit sign. If they could just get to it, get out of this museum, then they'd be able to get to Mustang and get the hell out of there.

Except for Bang Bang.

That hit Wyatt hard, but there was nothing they could do for him now. The only way they'd be able to help is if they made it out of this museum alive. So they ran, as hard as they'd ever run in their lives, directly for the exit. Toward freedom. They just had to—

"*Stop!*"

Mimic grabbed Roman's wrist, pulling him back, pointing upward.

A blinking light, just next to the red exit sign. Directly above them.

Wyatt barely registered what he was looking at before Roman pushed him to the side just as the bomb went off. It was close enough for Wyatt to feel the heat of it singe his eyelashes, burning the tips of his hair. He fell to the floor, coughing, trying to suck in a breath. His head spun, and his blood pressure

The Sunset Job

spiked. He struggled to get up, having a difficult time getting his legs to work.

Where was Roman? Mimic? He looked around, called out for them. They were just at his side...

The rubble next to him. A small wall had been constructed where there hadn't been one before, made of concrete and cement and tile and stone.

"Roman! Mimic!"

Please don't be buried under there. Please don't be—

"We're safe," Roman responded through a small fit of coughs. "Are you hurt?"

Wyatt looked himself over, taking quick stock. No blood, nothing impaled, nothing broken. "I'm fine, I'm okay." He managed to stand up, his shoulders beginning to shake. Dust filled the air, the coughs getting more intense, making his head hurt with the pressure. He wiped at his eyes, making the problem worse.

How was he getting out? He couldn't see the exit sign anymore. He'd have to turn back around, run through another section of the museum. He'd have to—

"Put your hands up, right fucking now. Now!"

Wyatt turned, staring directly down the barrel of a pistol, LAPD lining the entire hallway, blocking the only exit out of the tunnel.

Oh no...

Chapter 31

Roman Ashford

EVERYTHING WAS BLOWING UP, both figuratively and literally. Roman couldn't quite process just how fucked this entire job was. Light flickered above him as the door hung off its hinges, showing a clear route of escape that would take him into a back alley and out of the museum.

But it would end up leaving Wyatt inside. He'd already had to leave behind Bang Bang; he couldn't do that to another one of the Rainbow's Seven. "Go," he told Mimic, running in the opposite direction, following the small wall of debris to try and get to the other side.

"I'm not leaving you," she said, running at his side, face covered in dust. She wiped at her eyes, black nails coated in the same white debris.

The bomb had taken down a lot of the ceiling and piping, but it didn't extend down the entire hall-

The Sunset Job

way. They reached the end of the rubble and turned, placing them directly behind the backs of five LAPD officers, all of them with their guns drawn and aimed at a terrified-looking Wyatt.

Roman's heart plummeted. He couldn't let this happen. Not to Wyatt.

"Take cover. I'm going to draw them my way. You need to get Salt out of here. Whatever you do."

He took out his gun. Mimic's eyes went wide. She put a hand on his wrist, whispering, "Don't do anything stupid."

Unfortunately, Roman didn't have time to judge whether his plan was stupid or not. He needed to act before they slapped a pair of handcuffs on Wyatt and dragged him away.

"Just get him out."

Mimic gave his wrist a squeeze, her eyes projecting the mountain of worries that rose inside her. Roman mouthed an "I'll be okay" and motioned for her to hide on the other side of the rubble. She nodded, hurrying around the corner in a crouch.

And with that, Roman raised his gun and pulled the trigger. The bullet hit his target, tearing through an exposed pipe running directly above the police officers. Water rained down on them with a stinging pressure, causing four of them to turn and shoot in Roman's direction.

He hunched low and ran, running down the hallway back the way they came, toward the inside of the museum and away from his freedom. The four officers gave chase, shouting threats of more shots if Roman didn't stop immediately.

Of course, he didn't listen. He continued to run, exploding out into the Renaissance Hall and nearly knocking over a painting. Mimic could handle one officer; he just needed to keep the attention on him.

"Freeze!"

The shouts fell on deaf ears. Almost all of the museum visitors appeared to have been evacuated, which told Roman they wouldn't hesitate to take a shot if they had one. He wound through the paintings, making sure to keep as much cover as he could. All he had to do was buy time. That was all he really could do.

Fucked. This is all so irreparably fucked.

How had this even happened? They should have had the tome back in their hotel by now, all of them working together to crack the final code. How could he have overlooked Alecia? She was a blind spot that never should have been. Phantom always spoke so highly of her, had so much trust imbedded in their brother-sister relationship, Roman had trusted that to be enough.

He should have known that with Leonidas involved, enough would never be enough.

More gunshots rang out behind him. A bullet ricocheted off the far wall, a hole appearing where it had hit. Another went through the glass surrounding

The Sunset Job

a giant painting, the sound of clinking shards falling across the floor. He ran over them, glass crunching under his wingtips. He wasn't about to return fire, understanding the life sentence that would end up earning him.

He took a sharp right, running out into the concrete halls that were by the entrance of the museum. He could see the red and white lights from the police cars bouncing off the walls. The museum must have been surrounded by now.

Surrounded by police officers all told to look out for the Rainbow's Seven. They likely had clear descriptions of each of them by now. Roman expected SWAT to arrive shortly, cutting down any chance he had of escaping to nearly zero.

It wasn't there yet, though. He took another turn, away from the main entrance, running into a dome-shaped room with planets hanging from the ceiling, a constantly shifting view of the stars projected above him. He thought back to the maps he had made of the museum, remembering an exit past the infinity room, which should have been on the other side of this mini planetarium.

He ran, hard and fast. He had to lose these cops, had to get to Mustang. Then they'd regroup and figure out a way to rescue Bang Bang.

A fucking prison break. Great.

He'd worry about that later. "Stop right fucking now!" The shouting sounded closer, louder, enhanced by the acoustics of the room. His heart pounded with the force of a jackhammer. At least Wyatt would be safe, Mimic likely having already rescued him.

"Roman, where you at?" Mustang's voice sounded in his head.

"Do you have Salt and Mimic?"

A moment's pause felt like an eternity. "I do. Where are you?"

"Trying to get to you. I'm on the west side of the museum heading north."

"Got it. Just try and hurry, boss. This place is swarming with cops."

"I'm trying," Roman said, another gunshot going off behind him. A small podium exploded just to his left, sharp pieces of metal slicing into the back of his neck as he ran.

He didn't have time to even feel the pain. He ran into another hallway and made a right, running directly into the infinity room, seeing his reflection thrown back at him in a thousand different directions. He took a shaky step forward before hearing the police behind him.

Roman shot at the mirrors, his reflection cracking like a break in reality. He kept shooting as he entered the room, trying to look past the broken faces.

Another face filled the broken mirrors, and then another. The police were entering the room, guns held up and shifting between the reflections.

The Sunset Job

They must not be sure which one was the real Roman.

Good.

He pushed forward, trusting in his memory. There should be a small passageway that went through the maze of mirrors, leading to an exit on the other side. There were white lights all around, making it seem otherworldly, like Roman was running for his life through a field of twinkling stars.

There was a tragic beauty to the final moments of Roman's sunset job. It was meant to be the final one, the job that would allow him and his crew a life of unlimited luxury. He had envisioned a countless number of nights where he drifted around the Greek coast on his private yacht, looking up at a sea of stars, Wyatt curled up next to him and enjoying the same view, their heartbeats in sync and their legs tangled together.

"We did it, Salt."

"We did it."

"I love you. More than anything in this world. You're my everything, my fucking everything."

And then they'd devour each other as the waves gently rocked the behemoth boat, the stars only growing brighter and brighter as their sex lit the world on fire.

These weren't the stars he'd dreamed up. Far from it. This was a nightmare come to life.

There was still a chance for him to make it out,

though. That was all he had to do. Reach the exit. The police shouted from somewhere behind him, the four of them taking a cautious approach in entering the room. It gave Roman some much-needed time. He continued to run, his reflections appearing to be racing him, a sick game of outrunning yourself, the loser getting a life sentence behind bars.

Roman had no doubt that was what waited for him if he allowed the police to catch him. Leonidas had made sure to paint their hands red, fabricating evidence and planting those bombs to make it seem like the Rainbow's Seven were some kind of domestic terrorists.

And the world would believe it. It wasn't like Roman's long criminal track record inspired much confidence. He'd be fighting an uphill battle when it came to proving their innocence, but he'd make sure to fight tooth and fucking nail. If things came down to it, he wasn't going to allow the Rainbow's Seven to be looked at like they were some kind of monsters. He deliberately kept their hands as clean as possible, making sure that they tiptoed on the line between legal and illegal. Yes, they crossed over that line a couple of times but never far enough to get their names written on FBI's most-wanted list.

There! Directly ahead of him was a door, easy to spot since it stuck out against the walls of mirrors. He grabbed the handle, twisted, threw it open. Sunlight beamed into his face through a large

The Sunset Job

window. He was in another room, sans mirror, this one covered in flowers. There were vases overgrown with ivy, columns choked with the same, roses falling from the ceiling. The sweet smell of blossoms filled the air, doing nothing to calm Roman's pounding pulse.

He turned to the door marked as an emergency exit. He'd done it. He made it. Mustang would hopefully be waiting for him on the other side.

Roman bolted toward the exit just as the police officers burst into the room from behind him. More shouting, more gunshots. One of them grazed Roman's shoulder, miraculously only taking with it the fabric of his suit. He didn't want to keep testing his luck. One of these cops was going to land a shot, and they weren't shooting to subdue him anymore. They were aiming to kill.

He banged against the door with his shoulder, hitting the bar that opened it.

Fresh air smacked him in the face, mixing with the rancid scent of warming garbage. He was in an alleyway—no sign of Mustang. One way led him to a solid brick wall, and the other appeared to dump him out onto the streets.

There was only once choice to be made. He ran toward the opening, not even daring to look over his shoulder. Roman could practically taste freedom. He could feel the sparks on his skin once he had Wyatt back in his arms. That's all he wanted. To hold him again, to forget about this botched job, to put all his efforts into breaking Bang Bang out of prison.

He'd get to do none of that.

Roman ran out of the alley, out onto a side street lined with tall palm trees and police cars parked under each one of them. He had made a mistake. Had run directly into their hands. It was an army of them, all with their guns drawn, taking cover behind their cars. One of them spoke into the car's speaker, her voice booming.

"Put the gun down."

Roman had no choice but to listen. There was no running from this. The realization of that was heavy but quick, making him accept his immediate fate even though inside he felt like a caged animal, left with no food or water, banging its body bloody against the bars.

He set the gun down on the ground, moving slowly.

"Boss, everything okay? Where are you?"

"No, everything isn't okay," he said under his breath, mouth as dry as an ashtray. "I'm about to be arrested."

The officer stood up from behind her car, about a dozen others following suit. A trio of bomb squad vehicles pulled up, looking like tiny armored tanks. "Hands behind your head. Get down on your knees, or we will shoot. Don't you dare take another step."

The concrete was hard against his knees, a dirty

The Sunset Job

puddle underneath him soaking into the soft fabric of his pants. He lifted his hands behind his head, looking up at the sky before being surrounded by a mass of officers. The cold steel of the handcuffs cut into his wrists as he was dragged up onto his feet and escorted into the back of the nearest cop car.

That was it. The game was over, and Roman had lost. His mind whirred with a million different thoughts, but only one was loud enough to break through the noise:

At least it's me and not Wyatt.

Chapter 32

Wyatt Hernandez

It should have been me.

The thought played on a loop in Wyatt's head. It tortured him, growing louder and louder with every repetition.

Everyone in the van was silent as a dead rat. No one spoke, no one coughed, no one even breathed. They had fucked up, and they'd lost two of their own because of it. Roman and Bang Bang, both cuffed and jailed. Wyatt looked out the window, Mustang driving on the freeway as quick as she could, putting distance between them and the museum. The Hollywood hills surrounded them, like a physical wall wanting to further separate Wyatt from Roman.

It should have been me.

"Huh?" Mustang asked, knuckles pale against the steering wheel.

The Sunset Job

"It should have been me," Wyatt repeated out loud, the words strangled by a rogue cry. "Roman drew the cops off of me—it gave a chance for Mimic to save me, but it meant catching him. It should have been me."

"Really? So you think you'd be able to handle being taken into a maximum-security prison, being held with the worst of the fucking worst?"

Wyatt tried to answer but couldn't find the words. Or rather the word "no." He wouldn't have been able to handle that at all, but at least Roman would be out. The Rainbow's Seven wouldn't be missing their leader. He knew Roman would have a plan to get him and Bang Bang out by nightfall.

Instead, it was Roman behind bars, the rest of the Rainbow's Seven left out to dry. How could they come up with any sort of plan when their head was chopped off?

"Be grateful, Salt." It was Phantom, sitting directly behind him. "Roman did it to save you."

"I know, I know. I just... fuck. Fuck." Wyatt hit his head against the headrest.

"Can't we prove it wasn't us?" Doc asked. "We weren't even in California last night. Can't they look at our plane tickets and see it was a setup?"

Mimic shook her head, setting her phone down, images of the California State Prison taking up the entire screen. "I don't think the LAPD *or* the FBI are going to listen to a single thing any of us have to say. They've got video footage, and I'm sure Leonidas somehow got our DNA all over the bombs. Plus, the fact that we ran out of there doesn't help our case."

"So what do we do?" Doc asked.

More silence, broken by a curse from Mustang as she looked up, spotting a police helicopter, likely looking through the highway for a van matching the description of the one spotted darting away from the museum.

Too bad for the cops, Mustang had a replacement vehicle waiting for them. The switch had gone fine, their black van now a white SUV. Still, Mustang clearly didn't want to land on their radar. She took the next exit, landing them somewhere in the Valley.

Wyatt lowered the window and took in a deep breath. He had to fight through the darkness that clouded his thoughts. There'd be time later for sadness and regret, but right now, Roman and Bang Bang needed them. They couldn't act as if it was all over. Wyatt knew that wasn't how Roman would have handled the situation. He'd likely have ten different plans already drawn up, each one better than the last.

"We break them out." Wyatt answered Doc's question over the sound of wind rushing into the car. His shoulders weren't shaking, and neither was his voice. Maybe he could do this?

The Sunset Job

"How?" Mustang asked. "We're already wanted criminals."

"So that makes things easier for us," Wyatt said, finding more and more confidence with every word. "We've got nothing to lose and everything to gain. Logically, that's one of the best positions to be in."

"Logic isn't going to solve this one," Phantom said. "None of this shit makes any fucking sense." His jaw clenched, along with the fists balled in his lap. He must have been going through a gamut of emotions after finding out his sister was the one who'd betrayed them, and for reasons she couldn't really help. It was a twisted situation that would likely need years of therapy to get over.

Wyatt didn't respond to Phantom, his mind focused on the hundred different threads beginning to form one clear tapestry in his head. He understood how turbulent Phantom's emotions must have been and didn't blame him for that. Mustang also looked shaken, along with Mimic. Doc appeared composed but tight-lipped, shock likely filtering through her in a different way than the others.

Wyatt had to take the lead. In order to save Bang Bang and Roman, he had to step into his shoes. It would be a large departure from how Wyatt viewed himself, but that couldn't stop him from at least *trying*.

He sat up a little straighter in his seat. "Mustang, drive us to our hideout. Mimic, can you make some calls and find out exactly where they're going to be held? Discreetly, of course?"

"Sure thing." She pulled out her phone, opening up her infinite list of contacts and typing something into the search bar. Moments later, she had the phone up to her ear and was whispering with her contact.

"Doc, Phantom, either of you bring a laptop?"

Phantom nodded, leaning around his seat and grabbing a backpack. He handed the entire thing over to Wyatt, slumping back into the chair, a hand over his eyes.

"Thanks, Phantom." Before Wyatt grabbed the laptop, he turned and put a hand on Phantom's knee. "Your sister was manipulated into this, okay? If anyone's at fault for this, it's Leonidas. Once we've got Roman and Bang Bang back, we'll take the tome back and make Leonidas pay for everything he's done."

"That's a big fucking bill he's racked up," Phantom said.

Wyatt let Phantom simmer. He didn't want to push anything, not when all of their nerves were as frayed as they were. He focused instead on the computer in his lap, hooking it up to his phone's cellular connection and opening up a blank email. He typed in the address of someone he was sure he'd never speak to again.

The subject line was simple: I need your help.

The Sunset Job

Don't worry, Roman. We're coming for you. I'm coming for you.

Wyatt typed out a message and hit Send, the car once again slipping into a heavy silence, broken only by Mimic's newly accented voice asking for information regarding the arrests of Roman and Bang Bang.

* * *

Roman Ashford

Roman shuffled down the narrow hall, white concrete walls surrounding him, cramped. His hands were handcuffed in front of him, and he'd changed from the three-piece tailored suit to a baggy pair of orange pants and tan shirt, rough against his skin. He walked with his head down, avoiding making any eye contact with the men shouting from inside their cells. Some accompanied their curses and insults with spit. Others rattled the bars with their hands, banging their heads against the hard metal.

Roman stuck out like a sore thumb with his clean haircut and fit physique, his permanent baby face hiding the fact that he could hold his own against these men.

"Get in," the warden said as they reached an empty cell at the end of the row. Roman was unceremoniously pushed into the cell, the heavy door sliding shut and locking on its own. The officer motioned toward the cuffs. Roman stuck his hands out of the small opening in the door and let the officer release his wrists.

For a split second, Roman considered what would happen if he reached for the officer's shirt and slammed him against the bars. Could he muster enough force to knock the guy out? He might be able to reach for the keys, but getting out of the prison would be an entirely different obstacle.

He brought his hands back to his side, the officer shutting the small opening with another key before leaving Roman inside his new home.

He looked around, the gray walls scratched up and stained, some of it appearing to be dried blood. There was a small bed pushed up against the wall, the thin blue "mattress" exposed, also showing off a collection of different stains. There was a pile of scratchy white sheets set at the foot of the bed. To the left of that was the toilet, exposed and open, a tiny sink directly next to it. No mirror, no medicine cabinet, no nothing.

Roman was up a creek without a paddle in sight, a waterfall roaring ahead of him. He was fucked. Completely and irreparably fucked.

But at least it was him in there and not Wyatt. He found a sliver of comfort in that thought. Wyatt would have been chewed up and spat out ten times over before the day was done. At least Roman could handle himself, and if luck was on their side (not that

The Sunset Job

it had been up until then), Bang Bang might be nearby. If he could find him, get a message to him, then maybe they could coordinate a way to break out.

It was a big if. Made more difficult by the fact that he was being held in a maximum-security prison. No cafeteria time, no outdoor time, no way to get together with anyone else. He'd be under constant watch, for crimes he hadn't even committed.

Roman sat on the edge of the bed, the bed frame creaking as if it were seconds from turning to dust underneath him. There weren't any windows, just solid concrete, making it near impossible for Roman to keep track of time. He instinctively looked to his wrist—pointless since his watch was already confiscated and likely on its way home with one of the officers.

He lay down, putting his feet on the sheets. This was his nightmare scenario playing out in real life. Not only was he locked up, but so was his best friend, and he had no idea where his crew was or how they were doing. For all he knew, they could have been caught, too.

No, I refuse to believe that.

Roman couldn't swallow that image. He believed in them far too much. Each of them was strong in their own respects, but together, they truly formed an unstoppable crew. This would only be a speed bump for them. It had to be. Roman needed to believe that the Rainbow's Seven would figure it out. He had to imagine Wyatt—Salt—taking the reins where Roman had dropped them, spearheading the rescue mission. It was that hope that would keep Roman strong and centered. He needed to believe that Wyatt would be back in his arms by the week's end.

In the meantime, though, Roman would be working on an escape plan from the inside along with a plan for after they were out. His sunset job wasn't over, not by a long shot.

In fact, Roman felt as if the job had only just begun.

The End.

Thank you for reading *THE SUNSET JOB*. If you enjoyed the story then please consider leaving a review.

And make sure to pre-order book two, THE HAMMERHEAD HEIST, out August 19th!

Want more Max? Sign up for my newsletter and get access to a bundle of free short stories along with exclusive excerpts/passages and behind-the-scenes sneak peeks.

Tap here to sign up for my newsletter.

Be sure to connect with me on Instagram, Twitter, and TikTok **@maxwalkerwrites.** And join my Facebook Group: Mad for Max Walker

Max Walker
MaxWalkerAuthor@outlook.com

Acknowledgments

Thank you to my partner, Armando, for being the photographer behind the stunning cover and thank you to Vania for catching all the times someone's eyes changed color (and all the other inconsistencies that slip past me). Sandra, the incredible magician with words and owner of One Love Editing also deserves a big thanks for her work editing this book.

Also by Max Walker

The Gold Brothers

Hummingbird Heartbreak

Velvet Midnight

Heart of Summer

The Stonewall Investigation Series

A Hard Call

A Lethal Love

A Tangled Truth

A Lover's Game

The Stonewall Investigation- Miami Series

Bad Idea

Lie With Me

His First Surrender

The Stonewall Investigation- Blue Creek Series

Love Me Again

Ride the Wreck

Whatever It Takes

Audiobooks:

A Hard Call - narrated by Greg Boudreaux

A Lethal Love - narrated by Greg Boudreaux

A Tangled Truth - narrated by Greg Boudreaux

A Lover's Game - narrated by Greg Boudreaux

Christmas Stories:

Daddy Kissing Santa Claus

Daddy, It's Cold Outside

Deck the Halls

* * *

Receive access to a bundle of my **free stories** by signing up for my newsletter!

Tap here to sign up for my newsletter.

Be sure to connect with me on Instagram, Twitter and TikTok **@maxwalkerwrites.** And join my Facebook Group: Mad for Max Walker

Max Walker

MaxWalkerAuthor@outlook.com